Ancestors

Gladys Swan

Ancestors

Gladys Swan

SERVING HOUSE BOOKS

Ancestors

ISBN: 978-0-9971010-5-8

Cover art: "Moon Tree and Celebrant," painted by Gladys Swan, photographed by Monte Nevins

Serving House Books logo by Barry Lereng Wilmont

Published by Serving House Books
Copenhagen, Denmark and Florham Park, NJ
www.servinghousebooks.com

Member of The Independent Book Publishers Association

First Serving House Books Edition 2015

Sources:

The story of Richard Wetherill is from the biography by Frank McNitt: *Richard Wetherill —Anasazi: Pioneer Explorer of Southwestern Ruins.*

The story of Marietta Wetherill came from transcripts of tapes from the Oral History Library at the University of New Mexico.

The description of the Snake Dance came from *The Book of the Hopi* by Frank Waters.

There are two mountains on which the weather
is bright and clear, the mountain of the animals and
the mountain of the gods. But between lies the
shadowy valley of men.

—Paul Klee
Diaries 1898-1918

Wherever humanity has made that hardest of all
starts and lifted itself out of mere brutality is a
sacred spot.

—Willa Cather

To Monte,
a Renaissance man, a great spirit

I.

Chaco Canyon. Somehow he'd made it over the corrugated dirt road that threatened to shake loose what little brain he still had intact. Inside the Visitors' Center, Hawkins put down the last bills in his wallet for the entrance fee and tried to concentrate as the ranger, an athletic-looking blonde taller than he, showed him the various hiking trails and indicated the ones requiring permits. "I want a long one," he said, "that really takes you back in."

She smiled as though they'd struck a common cord. "Well, if you can do only one," she said, "this, to me, is the most dramatic. You have to climb." She looked at him. "It's a bit strenuous."

Did she think he wasn't up to it? If he looked the way he felt, no wonder. He brushed back his hair, unsure he'd remembered to comb it.

"Then from the Overlook you can see the actual plan of Pueblo Bonito, how extensive it is, where the kivas lie, the whole panorama." Her voice rose with an emotion that seemed more complex than sheer enthusiasm. "You can continue even higher, right over the top of the A mesa. Past the Jackson Stairway. You can see the footholds picked right into the cliff and how the Anasazi climbed right up the face of the rock." Her voice was a siren in his ears. "If you have the time, you can go to Pueblo Alto."

"Terrific. Just the thing."

He tried to hide his nervousness as she pointed out the trailhead and showed him where it led. And if he were back in time, she told him, pausing in the midst, she'd be leading a tour of Pueblo Bonito. An hour and a half. She'd take the group all through the major rooms.

No, he wouldn't be back in time. He was ready to tear the map out of her hands.

"I majored in anthropology," she went on, infuriatingly. "I could talk about the place for hours. It's such a mystery."

Mystery? He wouldn't touch it. He could barely emerge from the confused fog of his own brain. No mystery about the origins. Fortunately, a family with kids came up, sparing him further conversation. The ranger gave him his permit and pointed out where he could find a trail guide. On the way, he snagged a bottle of drinking water from one of the shelves. The trail guides were fifty cents. He had change enough for one.

He moved to the counter, where two young Navajo women were apparently in charge, one behind the cash register, the other sorting through a pile of books. One with glasses, the other without. Modern women—up-to-date, speaking Navajo to one another. He counted out the coins, then paused; he wanted them to shift gears and speak to him.

"Chaco Canyon," he said, searching for a question. "The Navajos—a special place for them, right?" The one at the cash register thought it over, then deferred to her companion, who gave a shrug and shook her head.

"Not exactly," she said. "It wasn't our ancestors who first came here. We came afterwards. We just lived on the land."

And you're still here, he thought.

"The Hopis, though, the Lagunas, the Zunis," she went on to explain, "still come here for ceremonies. For them, it's a sacred place."

Sacred, but not for those here. He looked from one to the other, as if he might read from their expressions something about his own situation. Navajos. What were they doing here if it wasn't their ancestors? At least they belonged somewhere, if at the moment only behind a cash register. Whatever else, their people had put down roots in this stony landscape. But he was a single reed, transparent, ready to be taken down in ever so slight a wind. Even if his grandma, Ruthie, had said once there was Indian blood in him, from somewhere way back, but what did that mean? Maybe these females were holding back on him, knew something they weren't telling him. The notion made him uneasy, even angry. Did they know anything about witchcraft? He scowled and turned away.

He left the Center and drove along the Chaco Wash to the parking lot below Pueblo Bonito, just before the trailhead to the Overlook. First he'd see what he'd be looking down at. He had the permit in his hand.

Put one copy of the permit in your vehicle, he read, *and carry the other on your person.*

An absolute requirement. Rules. As if it would make any difference what he did. Always follow the rules lest they get you into the army, where his brother had ended up. And what had happened to him over there in the desert, in Iraq? Didn't know and didn't care. He drank thirstily from the water bottle, then put it into his daypack and slipped it on. He hadn't eaten anything—the very thought of food was enough to turn his stomach.

The night before, he'd pretty much shot his wad, drunk a dozen beers, puked and staggered off to his truck, where he'd fallen into a stupor. He'd been rousted up by a car horn blasting savagely behind him, driving the sound into his head like spikes. He flailed awake, turned on the ignition, threw the truck into reverse instead of drive, then nearly threw himself into the windshield as he jammed on the brakes to keep from hitting the car behind him. With every cuss word he knew, he shot forward out of the loading zone he couldn't remember parking in, bumped down an alley, turned into first one street, then another, till he recognized where he was. Once out of town, he stopped at a gas station to douse his face with water and swill down a Gatorade.

It was sheer impulse that took him to Chaco Canyon. When he was in the eighth grade, Ruthie, who, with her sultry voice and deep-throated laugh, her cigarettes and her men, never seemed to be of the right material for a grandmother, had taken him there with his brother, Clyde. That was before the trouble he'd gotten into and all the people he'd disappointed in their efforts to get him out of it set him straight. Before he spoiled Ruthie's hopes for him, and his brother kicked him out for good. Before the hole he dropped into.

It was getting hot. Though he'd been chilled to the marrow from his night in the truck, things had warmed up now as it approached noon. The air held a kind of late summer largesse, though it was mid-October. Brilliant sun on the yellow leaves of the cottonwoods, casting light everywhere. It hurt his eyes. He rummaged in the glove compartment for sunglasses, found a pair with a cracked lens, put them on anyway, then stood for a moment trying to get his bearings.

Pueblo Bonito rose from the hill at his right. He'd be looking down at it. He tried to remember if he'd been there before. He couldn't anchor a set of impressions, but he was sure Ruthie must have led them there. He was a kid then, different. Seeing what? He could remember only a kind of eagerness, like that of a dog turned loose, exploring. And a certain surprise that people had lived here once, in what had become a barren waste, raised their food, carried on their lives. He picked up a guidebook from the box and walked up the path.

It occurred to him his feet had been the same size then that they were now; he'd reached his full growth by then, and would soon work up a hatred of school that made him squirm in his seat, ready to become a discipline problem.

A sign admonished him to show respect, that he was entering sacred precincts. Whatever that meant. Like a church, he supposed. After he left grade school, nobody tried to make him go. Ruthie herself admitted she never found anything in all that holy-moly stuff, just wasn't made for it.

Walls, thick walls, rose ahead of him. Pieces of brick worked together so skillfully, you could only wonder how they knew to do it. He'd done some construction work himself, but this was beyond his imagination. Walls, rooms and doorways. A maze, a continual set of intersections. One storey atop another. His head swam. He wouldn't go inside the rooms, just walk around the pueblo, then set about what he'd come for.

He headed toward the back near the cliff, where the great rock had towered over the village, had been a threat for decades; they'd known about it from the beginning, put their village there anyway, tried to shore it up. Half a century ago, it had finally fallen. He studied broken walls, the guidebook trembling in his hands.

12

He remembered the rock now, remembered saying, "Too bad they didn't have t.v. I'll bet it was a blast."

"They weren't even here then, Stupid," Clyde said, always the one to show him up.

"Fuck off."

"You don't talk like that here," Ruthie said with real anger. "You show respect."

For a bunch of old stones. The walls looked good for some climbing, if he'd dared.

"You boys ought to remember all this," he could hear Ruthie saying. "Who knows, maybe one of our ancestors helped build the place."

So if they did—nothing spoke to his blood. It all happened too long ago, and he'd been just a squirming thirteen-year-old. Though Ruthie had some memories of her mother and grandmother, she seldom spoke of them. She wouldn't even talk about his father, and precious little about his mother. But he didn't care. He and Clyde had shucked off history to leap over rocks and tear along the trail, till Ruthie yelled for them to get some sense in their heads or she'd make them go sit in the car. He'd spent here some of the last moments she'd had any real control over him.

Soon as he hit high school he was heading in the direction of trouble. Maybe because Clyde was so clean-living. True, he didn't do serious drugs. Just pot. He didn't get all that high because he didn't like the way the stuff burned his throat. Besides it cost money. Beer was more his style. He liked chugging it down, hanging out with guys a few years older who'd buy it for him. Not bothering to come home some nights. When he turned up, Ruthie beat him with her shoe if she could catch him.

Stealing didn't occur to him at first. He worked up to it, though what he took from Ruthie was in the family, so it wasn't anything. Nor swiping hub caps for a little spending money. He and the guys he ran with hot-wired a couple of cars and went joyriding just for kicks. But except for burning up the tires, they'd left them as they found them. And then when he, together with Cliff and Mackey, knocked off the convenience store, it was no big deal. They'd taken beer and snacks and done a little damage to say they'd been there. It was knowing he could do it that gave him the thrill. Knowing the danger and going ahead anyway. Getting all his senses poised and then the taste of freedom, the freedom he craved. And now that freedom had made the loop and brought him back to Chaco.

Ruthie, it was you started me on my way. So here I am, Ruthie. Back with the ancestors, if it's any comfort to you. Say I owe it to you. Looking to the right, he saw that the trail turned; the Petroglyph Trail, it was called, following a succession of petroglyphs along the face of the cliff. Pictures that meant something once—people still struggling to figure them out. He stared up at the top of the broken rock that threw its shadow over him. There were marks in it, but he couldn't make out any petroglyphs. Only the marks that wavered into images of what had brought him here to exercise his terrible freedom. The bar, Cliff, and what followed the ride out of town.

"Come on," he could hear Cliff saying. "Come on, we're going to have a little action."

It was an ordinary night. He'd started drinking around nine, after exchanging a few wisecracks with Seth, the bartender, and a new guy working with him, who'd moved down from Colorado. He was just getting into it when Cliff came in looking for him. He'd been drinking as well. Hawkins wasn't eager to leave, but Cliff kept at him, "Listen, you can't miss out. We got a good thing going."

Finally, he gave in and followed Cliff out to the waiting car that had been left with the motor running.

"This here's Drew," Cliff said, with a flip of the hand towards someone in the back. "Just got out of the army and wants to celebrate." Mackey was there, too, and another guy sitting between him and Drew.

"Who's that?" Hawkins said, as he slid into the front.

"Nobody—" Cliff said. "—a Navajo. Drunker'n a skunk. His buddy's back there." Cliff said. He pointed in the direction of the trunk and headed toward the driver's seat. Though Hawkins knew with sure instinct he wanted out, the car was already in motion, and it was all he could do to hang on and pull the door shut. The guys laughed. They rolled on through the streets to the edge of town, past the occasional lights of houses, and out into the land, radio blasting away. Then just before they turned down a ranch road, Cliff shut off the noise and crept along for a couple of miles.

"This should do it," he said, pulling to the side, shutting off the motor. Drew and Mackey hauled the Navajo out the car. A short, stocky fellow in jeans and checkered shirt, black hair braided. He stood there dazed, and woozy. Mackey shone a flashlight in his eyes, and Hawkins saw him struggle when he discovered his hands were bound and that he couldn't shield his eyes.

"Joe," he yelled. "Hey, where are you?"

"That your buddy?" Cliff said. "I'll give you some company so you won't get lonesome."

Cliff went around to the trunk. "Give me a hand,' he said to Hawkins, whose mouth had gone dry.

"Hey, get a move on," Cliff said, "You wanna spend all night?"

To keep his stomach from turning back to that moment, Hawkins tried to anchor himself in the guidebook. He moved slowly along the back of Pueblo Bonito. Here the walls were four stories high. He was taking a wide arc back to the entrance. No hurry—he had all the time in the world. He wound through a maze of rooms, then found himself at the plaza. Holes. Deep ones, with walls. He managed to concentrate long enough to read about the Great Kivas, to notice the benches around them, the fireboxes, the keyhole shape of one of them. Ceremonies in the dark with fires burning. Men climbing down on ladders, climbing back up. The holes looked to be twenty feet deep. If you fell in one, you'd rearrange a few vertebrae. He considered a moment. Would it kill you or just turn you into a human wreck? A shuddering thought—having to live with what you'd done to yourself. He caught sight of something down below, squinted: the skeleton of some small animal that had fallen in.

What could he have done—turned and walked off in the dark? That was it, he decided now—just walked away. Only he hadn't done that. He'd gone back to the trunk with Cliff and hoisted the guy out and onto his feet. He was a big man with a round heavy face, older than the other. They had to hold him up.

"Where'd you put their money? Drew said.

Cliff laughed. Right in the glove compartment—what they haven't drunk up. I'll bet it's a week's pay. They'll be looking a little grim tomorrow. Probably won't remember a thing."

The stocky one looked around, disoriented, shook his head as though to clear his vision. "Where—? You guys— What's going on?"

"You didn't have any money," Drew said nastily. "Wasn't worth our time,"–and kicked him in the groin. He fell over into a heap. Drew and Mackey kicked him a few times, hauled him up and threw him against the barbed wire fence.

Cliff had the other. "C'mon," he said, motioning Hawkins.

The three of them were dark shadows behind the flashlight, but Hawkins felt their contempt. "Let's see that kicking leg," Drew said. "I can show you a few army exercises to loosen it up."

His guts turned against him, and he bent over, stomach heaving. The three of them roared with laughter. "You'd do great on the front line," Drew said, giving him a kick that sent him sprawling. "They'd never work the chicken out of you."

"Leave him alone," Chris said. "Let's finish with them."

From where he lay, Hawkins could hear yells, groans. Then it was quiet. Cliff and the others walked to the car. He heard the car doors slam. The motor started up, and he was alone with the other two. He lay there for a long moment shaking with cold, then slowly rolled over and sat up. He didn't want the others to see him, didn't want to know what shape they were in. But he could see anyway, how their clothes had been had been torn by the barbed wire, how they lay cold and in pain on the rough ground. He staggered up the road till he reached the highway. A trucker gave him a lift back to town.

He left Pueblo Bonito and made his way to the trailhead, paused for a gulp of water before he started up the trailhead. Almost immediately, the climb began, and he could see the wash below, the brilliant tops of the cottonwoods. Soon he was at a narrow passage between two outcroppings, climbing and twisting his way between them. He paused, panting. He was out of shape and, as he climbed, the blood thrummed in his head. No wonder—the sort of life he'd been leading: working for a while so he could eat and pay the rent, hanging around the bars playing video games. When his money began to dwindle, he'd cap things off with a binge, as though to wipe away the loathing he continually felt. He didn't go to Ruthie's funeral. Afterwards, his brother found him and beat the shit out of him.

Things had gone much the same way till he met Aline. It was a wonder she had anything to do with him. He'd met her, of all places, in a bank. He'd gone up to a window to cash his check and found himself staring at one of the most beautiful young women he'd ever seen. He couldn't take his eyes from her face, it was so fresh and open, the expression so lively. He was immediately drawn to her, to some quality he wanted to roll in like sweet grass. "You new here?" he asked her.

"I've been here two months." She counted out his money, handed it to him.

"I think I need to spend more time at the bank—unless," he added, "I could see you sometime outside of it."

"I'm usually home," she said, "taking care of my little girl."

"You're married?" he said, disappointed.

"No," she said. "Not married."

Maybe it was because of the kid she didn't have guys giving her the rush. At first he starting picking her up after her work and taking her home. She rode in with the older woman she lived with. Weekends he could come to her place, where he tried to make himself useful. Chatted with her house-mate, if she was around, put his best efforts into making friends with two-year-old Sarah, who was shy and hung back at first. He brought her presents—a stuffed bear, a bag of blocks. Domesticity attracted and perplexed him, made him feel like some sort of savage. He had an impulse to put some order to his life, but it was as though he'd been handled a puzzle without instructions. Aline seemed beyond him; whatever had happened to her hadn't dragged her down, though she'd certainly had it rough.

She'd gotten pregnant her junior year in high school, and her folks had a fit. But she was determined to finish school and wanted to have the child. And no, she wasn't going to marry the father—it wouldn't work out. After the baby came, she moved out on her own. She was saving up her money to go to college.

He hid from her all he'd done to mess up his life. But he kept to his job, working for a building contractor. He avoided the bars where he'd hung out, avoided any contact with his old buddies, and only occasionally went for a beer with some of the guys he worked with. When he felt more sure of himself, of her, he started telling her how he'd gotten into trouble.

"I guess that makes us even." she said, "only it brought me something I can't do without," she said, putting her arms around Sarah and hugging her. "Give Mama a kiss."

"Then you can give me one, too," he said. "You know, the first time I saw you—"

He tried to find words for that moment, but what were words? He'd loved her immediately. It was what shone through her face, her every movement, that drew him, made him hungry with longing.

For the first time, he wanted to shed the life that stank in his nostrils. But he'd been making a shape in the configuration of things, and out of the corner of his eye he seemed to catch a glimpse of its shadow stalking him. Several weeks after the night he couldn't forget, a couple of police officers turned up at work and took him in for questioning. Fear froze him. Somehow the mischief he'd caused before had never caught up with him. But this time, Drew, Cliff, and Mackey had all been brought in on charges of robbery and aggravated assault. They'd been at it awhile, lying in wait for Navajos too drunk to know what was happening to them, then stripping them of their cash and torturing them. Cliff and the others were convicted and given stiff sentences.

By cooperating with the police, he drew a suspended sentence. Afterwards, he'd gone on a three-day bender himself. Aline would have nothing to do with him after that.

"You didn't tell me," she said. "That's the worst thing, deceiving me like that. It's a matter of trust; if you can't have that, what do you have? And then you go off and drown yourself. As if that was going to solve anything . . ."

She was all fire—a force of nature. He wanted just to stand there in the blaze and let it consume him.

"Look at her," she said, as Sarah followed their voices with troubled eyes, "You think I can let her put her trust in you? She's got a right to a future. I'm sure not going to let anybody mess it up for her."

"I'm sorry," he said. Worthless words.

"Sorry! Yeah, you're sorry all right. One big sorry mess."

Aline dissolved into his grandmother, Ruthie intoning the deep notes of her litany: "When are you going to put yourself together, boy? You can't live a life when you're all broken parts."

He had no argument to put in his defense. He was no better than his dog, Buddy, who knew he was doing wrong when he stole food, cringed with guilt when you scolded him, but never gave up the chance to do it again. At that moment with Aline, he was ready to get down on all fours.

Maybe Ruthie'd have gone on letting him torment her, but his brother had given him the boot. The parting was brief and to the point.

"You wouldn't shape up—now ship out. Mess up on your own."

And who could blame Aline?

He'd reached a level spot of the rincon and paused to catch his breath. He could have been climbing toward the top of the world, everything extending outward, upward. He took out the water bottle and drank deeply. His stomach still felt hollow; his head was a drum. Old Ruthie had it right. Keep on digging the same hole and pretty soon you had a direction, even a goal, because you couldn't find your way to any other. All the time scared as hell of what you were headed into.

The case wasn't closed. Drew's family had money and the three men had a sharp lawyer, who managed to find some technicality that rendered the trial invalid.

They were released after less than a year in prison. But several weeks later, when the news was out of the papers, Mackey was found dead in an alley, his face strangely bloated. An autopsy revealed nothing of the cause.

"There's something in the wind," Hawkins heard an old man in the Texaco station remark to the clerk, as he scanned the local paper. Those Indians don't take things lying down."

A month or so later, when Cliff was found dead in his bed, without a mark on him, Hawkins awoke to a sense of dread new to him. It hung over him like a dark swirling mass that moved beyond whatever he'd done or left undone and threatened to engulf him. The whole landscape of his inner life froze into a single unmoving frame. He was paralyzed. Six months passed and nothing happened. Drew had quietly left the area. But the dread hadn't left with him. Most days Hawkins slept—daylight was better than the dark. He got a job delivering pizzas so he would have something to do at night. And though he tried not to think about what was heppening, tried to keep himself occupied every waking moment, he couldn't help touching a current of premonition.

At first, they were unable to identify the man they found in a motel room in Bluff City, Utah, without any sign of violence on him —so the police report stated—but with his arms and legs strangely contorted. When the man turned out to be Drew, it was only what Hawkins could have predicted. Rumors of witchcraft had been circulating.

That put him next on the list—a marked man. He kept to himself, refused to talk to anyone, didn't leave the room he was renting. The landlady, who thought him "a nice young man," left him food. To his surprise, a fellow he'd treated with a sort of off-hand contempt in high school sought him out. "My uncle knows a medicine man down at Zuni," he said. "Can ward off spells. We'll take you there."

But he was too demoralized to make a move. A month passed. His money was all but gone. He couldn't run away—they could get him anytime, so why didn't they do it? *Get it over with*, he kept telling them in his thought.

Then, as the days and weeks passed, it occurred to him they

were maybe going to let him live and torment him by giving him his freedom. The more he thought about it, the more it seemed the greater punishment. He took temporary work with the highway department, holding up a sign that said, "Slow" on one side, "Stop," on the other. It was all he could do to stand on his feet. Nights he drank until he felt sleepy. But once his stupor gave way, his dreams were so filled with threat and upheaval they drove him into wakefulness.

Finally, he got fired from that job, too, and he laid around, shades drawn, hardly distinguishing day from night, not thinking past the moment when his money would again give out. When that happened, what then? His misery yielded up the only answer he could come up with. And it seemed almost a triumph—at least he'd be one step ahead of his tormentors.

The sign pointed to the Pueblo Bonito Overlook, and he turned down toward it, hiking over the great slabs of rock, at one point jumping over a crevasse to get down to the edge. And there he was. He could see all the way across the canyon, the whole stretch of sky and cliffs on the other side, where Pueblo Arroyo and Casa Rinconada lay, then down to the cottonwoods all along the wash. Above him the mesas continued, and the trail to Pueblo Alto.

At his feet was Pueblo Bonito. How extensive it was! Rooms and more rooms in a semi-circle around the plaza, with all the circles of the great kivas, except for the keyhole kiva, to hold how many people? Whole throngs, it seemed. Before he leapt down into the midst of it, his eye was drawn to every detail as though he were under some compulsion to fix it in memory. At first he hadn't heard it, but then he was aware of a voice breaking into the silence like some shrilling bird. He didn't turn around, but in a moment it was clear the voice was calling to him.

"Hey, down there. Hello, hello."

He turned then and saw a woman on the ridge above him, apparently measuring the distance between herself and where he stood.

"Do you think I can get down there?"

How would he know?

"I got here." he called back.

He turned back to the pueblo below.

"I don't think I want to jump that crevasse," she said, moving closer. "I don't think I'm strong enough."

"Then come around the other side," he said, pointing the way. He stood watching her slow progress.

"Think you could give me a hand?" she said, breathless. "I had surgery a while back. I don't want to strain anything."

He moved up to where she stood, held out his arm to steady her as she worked her way down to the edge of the Overlook. They stood side by side.

"Well, I made it," she said. "That's something at least."

He wondered how she had managed it at all, especially the narrow passage at the beginning. Her face was pinched, and in spite of her exertions, it had a hospital pallor. A shock of loose hair fell across her forehead. "There's hardly any meat on those bones," Ruthie would have said. "Arms skinny as chicken wings."

He could virtually see her ribs underneath her white tee shirt. As if ashamed of what she'd revealed, she turned her eyes away. He himself was none too steady. He felt dazzled and light-headed. Silent, they took their gaze in various directions. He tried to let go of her, as if she weren't there. And then he let go of everything. Looking out, it was as though the air had liquefied and some current had passed through. He heard a low thrumming that wasn't just inside his head. Drums, he knew he was hearing drums. And the shaking—that was rattles. The pueblo was no longer a maze of walls, an expanse of plaza, but had been transformed into a hive full of people. Old men and boys. Young girls and their mothers. Women with babies. Grandmothers. In their tunics and kirtles, their woven grass sandals.

Everything seemed poised at attention, waiting. And he waited, too, with drawn breath. Then the drums were in their midst, the shaking rattles. Dancers appeared, some with masks and feathers—beings emerging from the depths of kivas, not just men, though they were men, dancing, chanting. Wielding their whips, shaking their rattles. Drums beating, until the ground under them seemed the skin of a drum itself vibrating with their feet, so that earth and sky and everything between all seemed part of the dance. Everything sprang alive. The dancers, gods but only men, were dancing stone and plant and animal—dancing all the men and women and children who'd ever been—all the ancestors. Dancing so that it would all continue, so that the sun would come up and rain would fall and the corn would appear and ripen for another generation. No difference in past and future, nothing intervening between above and below, as they came together in a moment that was no-time.

Swept up in it, he forgot he was standing there, forgot who he was, everything dissolving into the space that took in all he saw. His mind seemed outside him, absorbed—he was down there with them, caught up in the rhythms of drum and chant and beating feet. Another creature entirely, as though he'd been caught up by those dancing beings, cracked open, some husk falling away to insignificance and the rest revealed as somehow more vivid and real, closer to life, than he had known. Then as the apparition faded and he found himself back on the mesa, he had no idea what had happened or exactly what he'd seen.

"Oh, look, there's a hawk," the woman next to him said. "They sure can sail, those beauties."

He was startled back again into her presence. He could see her now, a woman in her forties perhaps, dark-haired, who'd somehow managed to get there.

"A good sign," she murmured, still following the hawk. "Well, I made it here," she said once again. "It's something. I used to do a lot of climbing. "But it's a long time since I've done anything like this."

She made him nervous: if she gave out and fell into a heap, what could he do?

"There was an evil thing in this body," she said, with a gesture toward her middle. "Wanted to take over, take me with it. Those doctors took it out. Only they took part of me with it," she said harshly. "And I haven't got it back."

"How do you know?" he said.

"I just lay there knowing," she said. "They were fighting over me. I could feel them. One day the bad part was up, and the next day it was down. I haven't got the good part back yet. But I made it this far." It appeared she had to convince herself of something.

"Are you going higher up?" she said.

The question startled him. He, too, had made it this far and had no thought of going farther. It occurred to him now he hadn't yet taken his last step; he'd been caught by surprise.

He still hadn't had the chance to think.

"I can't get there myself," she said, almost as if she were pleading with him. "I got this far," she murmured under her breath.

He looked at her. "Yes," he said—a sudden impulse. "I'm going on up."

She brightened. "Could you do me a favor?" She was fumbling in her pocket.

She put a stone into his hand. "I know it's stupid," she said, "but I had this idea. I don't know— I just wanted to take it up to Pueblo Alto, find a good spot for it there."

He held it up to the light.

"Pretty, isn't it? It changes—sometimes it looks red, sometimes violet. Could you do that for me?"

"If I can make it," he said.

"Thanks," she said. "I appreciate it."

She lingered a moment to gaze down at Pueblo Bonito, then left him, working her way slowly back up the rocks to the path. At the top of the ridge, she turned and waved. He was again alone, though he could hear voices coming up from along the trail. Something still held him to the spot, but he had to leave before someone else got there. He didn't want to talk to anybody. His hold on things was still shaky, though he was feeling a bit steadier, could maybe do it, actually make it to Pueblo Alto. And what for? To take a stone up there—a strange thing to be doing. But she had entrusted him with it, whatever it meant to her. She'd picked it up God knows where, probably didn't even know what it was. But she'd put something onto it, like it would make all the difference, though why it should be important to him he had no idea. He knew only that a charge had been laid upon him, and he had to attend to it, concentrate on getting there and finding the right place for what she'd given him. Maybe put it in a window or a doorway where the light would hit it. But he couldn't know till he got there. He had no idea whether it would make any difference—what was being offered or what he might be taking back; whether it was possible for him to live. He'd have to wait and find out.

II.

He must have wandered for hours. Suddenly he was wrenched from whatever state of unconsciousness he'd fallen into, as though a small explosion had occurred inside his skull. He sat up quickly, so suddenly his head reeled. It was a moment before he could find his focus, shake away whatever had come to him, whether out of the sleep that had overwhelmed him, or something else that had stood at the edge of it and approached the vessel of his mind. He'd heard a voice in his sleep, and something pulled him toward the unfamiliar. And a declaration, almost a litany kept running through his head: *I was with him when he saw it*. But whether it was really a voice he'd heard or something made up out of his own head, he couldn't say. But whatever it was made him edgy. He shook his head to clear the static in his brain.

He had been lying in a scrunched up position on the ground, one arm pinned under his body. It felt as though it didn't belong to him, and he stretched it out, stretched his fingers to get the circulation back. His legs were stiff. The stony surface where he lay had made him cold, and his bones ached. Except for these sharp reminders of his physical body and its condition, he had no idea where he was or what amount of time had passed. Like getting drunk, with none of the pleasure.

He could see the sun descending behind the mesa, and each moment confirmed the receding color in the landscape, the gathering chill. A solitude so complete overcame him his consciousness faltered before it.

He tried to orient himself. Where had he been and where was he now? He lay on a stretch of buff-colored rock with the buttes rising beyond, ochre, rinsed in shadow. All he could remember was the climb upward. He'd been looking for the way to Pueblo Alto, but he couldn't find it. He'd gone past the Jackson Staircase. Yes, he'd seen the toeholds pecked into the side of the butte. Clever of them. He'd gone on and on, wearily, hardly knowing what he was doing until it occurred to him he'd lost the trail and was on the edge of nowhere.

He looked around, trying to focus, trying to get his bearings. Rock and dry grass and sage, mesquite and scrub cedar. Where had he got to? As he picked himself up, a sudden vertigo seized him, and he had to wait until it passed. His stomach was hollow, his throat dry. He pulled off his pack for the water bottle, swallowed the last of his water and tried to fight off a sense of panic.

He was wide-awake now in a time growing late. The trails would be closed before sunset. No use wandering over the top of the mesa. It would just take him farther away from the canyon. His only real chance was to head toward the edge of the mesa to see if he could pick up the trail. He started up. The sleep had given him back a few of his scattered resources, enough, he hoped, to get him down below to Pueblo Alto, back to the trail to the Overlook.

The woman had been the source of his trouble. How had she ever managed to get up where he was, scrabbling over the rocks? She looked like a slight breeze would take her up like dandelion fluff. And what had made him take her stone? Yet it bothered him that he hadn't gotten her stone where she wanted it to go. He had let her down. Crazy that it would matter to him. He paused for a moment. What was he getting into? How would she even know whether he'd gotten it up there or not? Crazy. Had she put some kind of spell on him?

He looked around. That high on the mesa it was like walking on the floor of the upper world. Himself and the sky, as though it would reach down and float you up into one of the cloud patches. He could see out across the wash and below to another of the ruins, though he didn't know which one. He started working his way down a series of ledges, skirting the lichen-covered rocks as he went. A single glance down on what the millennia had taken for the lichen to form there in a patch of color. But he had no time for distractions. His eye was everywhere. He saw what looked to be the trail and followed it till it petered out in a patch of brush. His legs ached and his knees felt wobbly. He wanted to weep from tiredness and pain. If he came to the edge he could just throw himself over, as he'd intended to do. With a sense of joyful release. Out of his body. Out of torment. Sail over the edge in one giddy moment of freedom. Wasn't that what he'd always been looking for?

And he was getting closer to that moment. But he felt something holding him back, not just a hesitation, but a great resistance. He couldn't understand. He wasn't in the same place he'd been. Because of the stone in his pocket? He could take it out and throw it to the ground, and what difference would it make? But he was compelled to feel around for it in his pocket. Not there? He was caught by the fear it had fallen out when he dropped down to sleep. But there it was—he had it. He felt an inexplicable relief. He took it out, looked at it, let the light work through it before he put it back.

He pushed himself onward. Up ahead he saw three buzzards circling, and paused for a moment to see where they were headed. "Piss off," he told them, "I'm not dead meat yet." Greedy bastards. Always looking for the next meal. Only their meals were always free, a really free lunch. He remembered once coming across a dead cow, a buzzard sitting on her head, dipping its beak into her eye.

Suddenly there it was—one of the cairns marking the trail. He looked ahead and lit on another. He saw now that he had entirely left the mesa where the Overlook had been and continued on over the bluffs to the mesa beyond. He was passing the Jackson Staircase with the footholds carved into the cliff, like a ladder up into the sky. He must have wandered miles. Miles that lived in the ache of his bones, a continuing reminder of how out of shape he was.

Now there were people. A heavy-set middle-aged couple, their broad faces pink with sunburn, both wearing daypacks, the man with a camera strapped at his side. They were descending from the trail that, so they told him, made a loop over the top of the mesa he'd just come from. They'd been hiking all day, but there was a brightness in their expressions as though the exertion had not only invigorated them, but liberated them. They, too, were headed back to the campground, eager for food and rest.

"I was trying to get to Pueblo Alto," Hawkins told them as he followed them downward along the trail.

"You can get it from up there where we were." But if he continued on down he'd see the sign. Slowly he made his way. The couple still had it in them to outpace him and were some distance ahead of him now.

Half an hour later, he saw ahead of him a trail that led upwards to the right, at the fork, a sign pointing to Pueblo Alto. He must have been blind to miss it. Perhaps so absorbed in what he'd just been seeing, what had prevented his downward leap, he'd gone right past. Or the woman. He couldn't get her off his mind. Ruthie had been like that towards the last. Struggling between life and death. Cervical cancer—only it had gone too far, reached up into other parts. The last time he'd come around he could see she was beyond the point of turning back, though she insisted she was making progress, had got to the other side of things now. He knew that she knew. He couldn't do much except smile dumbly, unable to think of anything to say.

He hadn't gone around to see her again, couldn't take to her the mess he was. Couldn't bear to remind her of it. Not when she was so close to the edge.

So now he'd have to go down and find somewhere to spend to night. At least there was a campground at Chaco. He had a sleeping bag in the truck and a tarp to keep off the rain those times he slept in the truck bed or at a campground. Those times when his money gave out and he got evicted from wherever he was living. But he had no money for the camp fees, and they'd very likely run him off if he tried to park by the road.

He considered the alternatives and let them slide away as he hiked past the Overlook. A couple of young men stood there, perhaps the last of those headed down. And once again he went down to view the panorama. Still a number of people were walking through the pueblo below. There till just before the park closed. His legs felt as if they might buckle out from under him. He approached the most difficult part. Carefully, he worked his way down through the passage between the boulders, a little easier going down now than climbing up those rocks. Then with a final effort, he was there, still intact.

But he still had the stone. Or else it had him. For he knew that he couldn't leave the canyon till he'd done with it—gone up to Pueblo Alto and put the stone where she'd asked him to take it.

He drove back to the Visitors' Center. Just outside was a water tap where he could fill his bottle. At least he'd have water. He was almost past hunger now, he was so enclosed with weariness. He would have been glad to throw his bones down anywhere.

Because it was the only thing that offered, he drove up to the campground, stopped and read the instructions. Ten bucks to stay the night: just fill out the form, tear off the tab to identify your campsite, put the money in the envelope provided and drop it in the box. Ahead of him he saw a fellow emerge from a trailer. He heard a deep voice. "Have a pleasant stay now." The door then closed behind him.

Hawkins went over to the door and knocked. He appeared once more, a large man with ruddy cheeks, grizzled hair and beard. He was wearing a red and brown checked shirt with suspenders. The Camp Host, according to the sign on his door.

"Welcome to Chaco," he said with an unfamiliar accent and asked Hawkins what he could do for him. From within came the odor of food cooking. A stew maybe. Hawkins' stomach growled.

"I got lost," Hawkins explained to him. "Up there on the mesa. I don't know how long I wandered around. It's getting late and I'm beat out. Could I stay here tonight?"

"Sure, man. Plenty of spaces this time of year." the host said with a sweep of fhs hand, giving him the run of the place.

"Trouble is, I don't have a cent."

"Well that's a pretty pass, isn't it?" The host looked him up and down, taking his measure. Scruffy, shaky, about to fall over, he could hardly stand up to any inspection. "What are we to do with you?" The tone suggested a real question—there were rules, and what was his authority? But a certain ironic, almost amused, speculation moved behind it.

Hawkins stood there, stripped bare before all those who had the right to be there by virtue of ten bucks. *The folks here are paying folks,* he could hear the host saying, *And you don't fit the description. Better be on your way, fellow.*

He looked up into his face and watched the host's expression open into good-humored largesse.

"Well, I would say there's a lot of empty spaces, and I don't know as 'twould do any harm. You'll be my guest. I'm the Camp Host, after all." He gave a laugh. "Just fill out the envelope and just drop it into the box. Post the tab at your camp site."

"Thanks a lot," Hawkins said, "You've saved me, man." and turned to go.

"You'll be needing some firewood—there's likely to be frost tonight."

"I didn't bring any with me." Hadn't thought he'd need any.

His host came out of the trailer, stooping a little, walking with a slight limp as he led Hawkins into the yard where his own wood was piled. He picked up a bundle wrapped in plastic. "Newspapers and kindling inside. And matches. Wait, I'll give you some extra kitchen matches." He went to the trailer to fetch them, and when he returned, wished him a good night.

Hawkins drove his truck around the camping area, looking for a spot out of the wind. Each site, he saw, was equipped with a picnic table and a round iron grill topped with a grate. He could sleep in the truck or else he could put his sleeping bag back against the face of the cliff along the outer edge. He saw just what wanted, parked the truck, and laid claim to his territory. Other campers were already settled in on either side of him, tents up, fires going, preparing supper. He parked the truck, went off to the men's room.

When he came back and looked around him, he saw that the bluff had an overhang, and below it was the façade of a small house. He could sleep there out of the wind. A stroke of luck. He followed the short path up to the dwelling, an ancient ruin, a farmer's house, a sign informed him. Behind, the ground was soft, sandy. Perfect. He went back to the truck for his sleeping bag and pad, got his flashlight out of the glove compartment, and laid things out behind the little ruin.

Returning then to the campsite, he set about starting a fire. He crumpled up the newspaper, laid the sticks of kindling across it teepee fashion and lit the match. Though the paper flared and seized on the kindling, it fizzled out before he could get the log to burn. Twice more he had to start the fire. "Damn it," he said. "Is everything against me? Haven't I made enough fires?" Once he'd set one against a garage on the alley past Ruthie's place. It left a scorched place on the outer wall, but that was all. At that moment, he'd have been glad to burn down the neighborhood. Finally, this one caught, and for a time he stood near the fire soaking in the warmth.

It was six-thirty, just at sunset. The light had already left the canyon, so that the lights of the campfires glowed here and there, small stations of warmth. He could hear laughter, kid noises, and the murmur of voices. He stood outside of all that. He watched his neighbor, an older man stirring something in a pot on a sizeable camp stove set atop one end of the picnic table. Soon they would be eating. They had all come there with food.

To the west were glowing coral-colored clouds, slowly paling against a paling sky. He sat for a while at his picnic table, watching the fire, toasting himself on one side, then the other, getting the benefit of its warmth before he turned in for the night. On the other side of him, a young couple was cooking steaks and playing a radio softly. The air was pure and chill; stars were coming out. A nearly full moon sent a glow down the rocky ledge in front of him, under which he would be sleeping. Beyond it, an indigo sky.

He wasn't sleepy yet, just bone-weary. But gradually the warmth of the fire soaked into him, and his eyelids grew heavy. He made a trip to the men's room to the toilet and the wash basin. He tried to rinse away the sour taste in his mouth, wished he had a toothbrush. Taking his flashlight and bottle of water from the truck, he walked the path back up to his shelter. He slipped into his sleeping bag, folded his jacket under his head, and gave himself up for the night.

He lay alongside the little dwelling just by a break in the wall that created an opening, whether by chance or design, it was hard to say. Maybe a small enough person could have crawled though it. Through it he could see stars, more stars than he'd ever seen, and closer. No lights from a town to compete.

He thought he heard coyotes in the distance, brought out perhaps by the moon. Suppose, he thought sleepily, you could go and howl with them, see how it felt. He was drifting. He saw one of the stars wink, come closer, and then the voice came to him again:

I was with him when he saw it.

Go away, he thought. What is this? He turned over to get away from whatever it was. Let me sleep.

You've slept enough of your life away already, the voice admonished him. *Only now . . .*

Rage jerked him up. " Look—if this is some kind of joke."

Patience, the voice told him. *I've come . . .*

"I just want to sleep, damn it. Why are you messing with me?"

. . . because you called. A chill went through him. Night was all around him. And he could hear the coyotes. "I never called anybody," he said. "You've got the wrong number."

Your heart called, though maybe you didn't notice.

Bullshit, he wanted to say, unable to imagine that any part of his body would go ahead without consulting him. Unless, of course, he was drunk.

You left a space big enough to drive your truck through. But it doesn't matter. Maybe you came looking for me. And I found you. Maybe we were both looking.

There was a silence, and Hawkins lay down again, wondering what had startled him up from sleep—what crazy dream. He had just about dropped off when the voice was in his ear again.

It was a blizzard. Snow coming down so thick you could barely see through the whiteness of it. Like a curtain in front of you. Richard and me, we'd gone out together to round up whatever cattle we could find that had scattered during the storm.

In spite of himself, Hawkins had to listen.

Hard going and fierce cold. We were there in the canyon, the wind swirling over our heads, and then there it was, ahead of us, something rising up out of the rock. High up there. And as we looked though the snow, it took a shape, a stone shape, storey upon storey of it. Up there in the cliff. People had come and made a palace for themselves, piled stone upon stone. Room upon room, doors . . . windows. It rose before our eyes like a vision behind that curtain of whirling flakes. That was how it began.

"What began?"

He vowed he'd come back when spring came. His life began in that moment. Began what would be his life. His fate. For Richard—for us all. I was with him when he saw it.

What was all that about? Hawkins was thrown for a loop. "Here, somewhere else? And who's Richard?"

Oh, now you want to know, the voice said, on the verge of laughter.

Rage went through him again, for he was wide-awake to something uncanny that was playing with him. It was so dark now that the stars were brilliant and dense. A profound stillness lay over the campground. He closed his eyes and waited for his head to clear. What had let in this craziness?

Now they call it Mesa Verde.

He'd heard of it, but he didn't know anything about it. And who Richard was he had no idea. Or whose voice he was hearing. He lay down again in search of sleep, but now his mind was a stream of images. He could have been there in that blizzard himself, on horseback riding out for the cattle that had strayed and stumbling on the unexpected. Whatever had opened itself to discovery. Like something out of a dream. He could see it, those stone dwellings high on the cliff, speaking of those who had been there who knows when. And who were they?

Ancestors, the voice said, as sleep overtook him.

III.

It was barely light when he awoke, and for a moment he had to call himself back into his body from wherever he had strayed. While he lay exhausted on the edge of sleep, another part of his mind seemed to open, a part that, until lately, he hadn't known existed. A blue space like a piece of sky. This time disjointed words, phrases, incomprehensible to him, came through like static. Then a sentence: *We sat in a circle and all joined hands. In the center it began.* Then something shifted, and he was back to himself. He felt divided. A part of him wanted to reclaim the blue space that was his mind but that didn't quite belong to him. The rest of him drew back.

He began to make out the dim outlines of the little dwelling, the jagged shape of the window he lay beside, the pale light that made its shape. It was cold around his head. He remembered that the camp host had spoken of a frost. He sank down again, to give himself to sleep. It was too dark, too cold to face the day and what the day might hold. He didn't want to think about it.

Do you have nothing—do you belong nowhere?

It was hovering over him, the voice in his ear, out of some dream perhaps. He turned over on his other side, hoping to elude it.

Once there was a boy who had a father but no mother. He didn't know what "mother" meant, why he didn't have one. Perhaps she was in the clouds with the spirits. Perhaps she had gone away and dwindled into her loneliness like a dried up sunflower. Perhaps she made a pact with the spirits of the bottle. His father couldn't take care of him. He was sick and weak. There was no food, there was nowhere to go. Did the boy have nothing, did he belong nowhere?

It was like a riddle he had been given, but he had at the moment no answer. *Nothing—nowhere* echoed in his mind. Whose story was it? It wasn't his, not exactly, but something like. And if there was an answer, it was no, there was nothing. And where was he to belong? His answer was silence.

How come you have no words? the voice taunted him.

"I don't know," he said. "Just let me alone, damn you."

Do you know what a stone is?

Questions being piled on him. Was there no peace? He sat up again.

"Why are you digging at me?" Fear overtook him. Maybe he really had gone out of his head.

Because you called.

He was in the middle of a nightmare, though the daylight beyond his shelter was beginning to suggest the coming of the sun. "I just want . . . a way out." He'd scraped the bottom of the pot—he couldn't think beyond the moment, the empty moment.

There's also a way in, the voice said firmly, as though it could see into his mind. *There is always a way.*

He sighed and gave himself up. "I have nothing," he granted. "I belong nowhere."

There was a little laugh. *Then you have room to fill with something.*

The birds and squirrels had it better.

Only listen, the voice suggested.

He could hear the throbbing of the wind—it had room, too, to roam in. A great emptiness.

There's the stone, remember.

Yes, the stone around his neck. Let him get up there right away, take it where she wanted it to go, and be done with it.

Do you know what a stone is?

A dumb question. What was he, a geologist? "Okay, the little hard pieces on the ground, made of minerals," he didn't know what. What was a stone? Some came round, others sharp; white and black, yellow and red, shiny and dull. A thing you cast at someone you wanted to hit or kicked as you walked along—except for that fool woman, who'd picked one up and kept it until she had somebody to put it on to—him. She was probably nuts. The world was full of them, stones and nuts.

You have work to do.

Okay, so he had to take the fucking stone up to Pueblo Alto. Let him do it. He couldn't lie there any longer.

You think you can just go and do it? the voice ragged him. *What's your promise worth when your thoughts are heavier than rocks? No good. Do you know why she's sending you?*

He hadn't a clue. He wanted to object, but he'd been caught out somehow. He'd been snagged by a promise, but now there were obstacles in his path, a blank wall everywhere he turned.

Either he went his way or yielded to the uncanny presence that had seized upon him. He was like jelly. He pushed up out of his sleeping bag, put on his jacket and headed toward the men's room. "I've got to take a piss—do you mind?" He saw that the windows of his truck were covered with frost, and he was grateful for the heat inside the men's room. After he'd relieved himself, washed his hands, dashed cold water on his face, he went out to try to take hold of the day. The sun was up now, and he looked toward it gratefully. The wind was chill, but the day promised to warm up. What next? He could get into his truck and drive somewhere— over to Chama maybe or down to Taos. See if there was any work. But in October the chances were slim, the height of the tourist season having passed—and the stone hung over him. He had to get rid of it.

He walked slowly back to the overhang to collect his stuff and put it in the truck. If he couldn't leave, would he be able to stay? There was no point in starting a fire since he had nothing to cook, and it would use up his wood. "So now what?" he asked, but the voice was silent—maybe for good—and he felt oddly alone with his own decisions. Perhaps he'd offended it. He paused, an echo in his mind. Nothing and nowhere. Was he to be haunted anyway? The Visitors' Center was somewhere at least, so he drove up to it and filled his water bottle. He couldn't do without water—it was something.

He saw that the Center was just opening and he was moved to go inside, if nothing else, to keep warm. He found a different person behind the counter, a young guy dressed in khakis, part of the Park

Service, who asked if he needed any help. Hawkins looked at him—clean-shaven, amiable and in charge. "No, I don't think so. " What had put him there to make the offer? What did *help* mean? "Have you seen our museum?" the in-charge guy asked him. "It's right along that wall, if you're interested."

He guessed he'd been helped. It was, after all, a way to kill time. He looked at the black on white pottery that had been excavated from some of the dwellings, large cylinders and bowls. Designs and patterns he'd never seen before. Toys in the shapes of little animals and birds. They'd taken mud and made these things, whoever they were, and put those zigzags and rectangles and circles on them. They'd put on the vessels something that told you of themselves—that sent archaeologists hunting for labels and explanations to put on little cards. He could see some kid holding his clay bird or prairie dog, making up a story in his head. He looked at arrowheads and tools. They'd hunted for food and cooked their meals and lain under the plastered ceilings of the great hive in this canyon. In this isolated spot. He wandered from the little collection to the bookstore, and browsed among the shelves. He picked up a booklet about the petroglyphs on the canyon walls and glanced through it. There were petroglyphs on the brief trail from the Center and others on the trail branching off from Pueblo Bonito.

Now you can make a beginning, The voice was in his ear again, just over his shoulder. He felt a curious relief, as though he'd not been abandoned, and though he had no idea where he was going or what difference it would make, he was not alone.

"I'm game," he said. "I've got nothing better to do."

You better believe it,

He didn't give any lip. He gave a nod to the fellow behind the counter, left the Center and drove down the loop to Pueblo Bonito, walked up the trail to where it branched off to Chetro Ketl and picked up a guide to the petroglyphs. It was different this time. No amount of goading would have sent the thirteen-year-old kid in the direction of knowledge. Maybe because there was always somebody trying to kick his ass. He had to show them they had nothing worthwhile to tell him, make it clear how boring they were. Video games gave him another world with adventures that tested his ability to be master of his fate. He lost himself in the conflicts between those bent on bringing disaster to the world and those who tried to defeat them. His blood rose, an excitement filled him. Monsters that threatened with their dragon bodies and poisoned tongues created some of the best excitement of his life. Action, conflict, drama. His imagination was quickened.

He continued the drama during his classes, falling away from the book in front of him, losing himself in the battles he replayed with their close shaves, momentary defeats and renewed dangers—taking sometimes the hero's role, sometimes the villain's. He reveled in diabolical cleverness. It didn't help his grades.

Now, too, he had entered into another world, this one like a bewildering puzzle. It was strange to be spending his time walking along the great cliffs from one marker to another, trying to locate the images, high and low, that had been incised in the rock. What were they to him? Some were very faint, and he had to strain to see them. Strange animals: some with two sets of legs and horns; others with four legs, one behind the other. He stood before them wanting them to deliver the goods, tell him the story. They made him impatient. What were they? What did them mean anyway, teasing him as they did out of some dim gone-by?"

Just look without reaching for anything and let them speak to you, the voice said maddeningly. *Don't reach for answers—there aren't any. Enter the dream. See with the eye of the heart.*

The dream. The eye of the heart. He wanted the push away what sounded like nonsense or something you'd see embroidered on a pillowcase. He hated that sort of shit. And the images—something like a kid might draw, yet they captured his eye with an unexplained power. Perhaps it was a dream, the place where you needed to enter—the doorway the blue space made that both invited him and made him anxious. As if at a sudden signal, the walls and outcroppings gave all sorts of images to him. As if with a curious sort of revenge. Meaning he wanted, was it? The cliffs were alive with creatures—

snakes and desert rats, deer and elk. He saw birds, a centipede. A whole stream of life swam giddily before his eyes. Then he saw other figures on the walls—wheels and spirals. Sun and moon.

The animals they hunted, the journeys they took, the clans they belonged to—the sun that warmed them, the night sky with moon and stars. Signs of their experience—that Spirit gave them. Now you have to take it as your own. That's their meaning.

A large ignorance pressed upon him. Experience—his own. Had he had any experience? The word puzzled him. He'd done things; things had been done to him. But he had no idea what to make of any of it. It had gone right through him—until the night that had sent him into the pit. Only he'd made some kind of mute appeal to Aline and Sarah to take him out of the misery of it. He wondered what was experience, when you knew you'd had it. His experience, and what the dwellers here came to before him—those who'd once lived and gone. He didn't know if he could in any way touch their experience. It belonged to another world, and they had been inside it. He stood on the outside. It was a ladder to climb, and he stood at the bottom, an alien.

And what were the eyes they saw with?

Again the riddle. The question you could keep on asking. People would continue suggesting this and that. And he would take away the images, an impression. They weren't his ancestors, the tribes who'd lived here. Only how could he say they weren't? Or what ancestors they went back to. Did it matter? He could almost see a stream of people from different tribes and times coming past, carving into the rock the news of their days, where to find success in the hunt, where they'd gone to plant their crops. He could see them cooking their food, the smoke blackening the vigas of their ceilings, as they sat before the fire telling their stories. Had they met an enemy or a friend? What game had they killed? He could see night coming to them. Stars, a whole skyful. And the moon making its rounds, speaking of time. Time for planting their corn and squash. Waiting for the right days for gathering and hunting and feasting. Dances for rain—it was a dry place. But that seemed only the outer shell of events. The rest lay behind it, like the life that had gone on in the little house he slept behind.

But one thing he did know. Whatever he had seen, whatever impression it had made, he could tell that he would not be allowed to dismiss the life that had been lived in the canyon. Or what was happening to him.

It's all here. The vibrations are still in the air. Their energies—Spirits.

"Spirits. You mean ghosts?"

Those who came before—they're still here.

"To haunt me?" He heard laughter.

You could say that.

And here, he thought, was one of them—who must have come through a doorway that somehow opened. How come this one had stayed with him and not gone back into the dream?

Then he saw something else. Faces. The face of a child formed by the rocks, an anguished child. Small—yes, looking out as though on a world it couldn't comprehend, lost, without a home. Then another face from the rocks—a face with smooth cheeks and eyes that looked on everything without flinching. The mouth was made of a little jutting rock. At first it seemed neither male nor female, but then he saw from either a shadow or a projection of a rock what seemed to be the smile of a woman. But no one had made these— they were tricks of his mind. Yet they belonged to him and held him, as though he had entered some part of the world being depicted here.

He was standing on the edge of a chasm that had opened in front of him. A false step might be fatal. The world he knew was dissolving. He stood now in a space between dimensions. No place for him to run and hide. And if he fell in? Terror seized him.

You'll come back to this place knowing.

Did he want to know? What would be required of him? What would he have to pay for it? He didn't feel exactly reassured. But he wasn't given time to worry over it. Another path lay before him.

You're near the place where you must enter. Like those called here before you. Those closer to you that you can recognize.

41

Now he had to go to the other side of Pueblo Bonito, where the trail led him away from the ruins for perhaps a quarter of a mile. On the way he startled up a flock of gray crested birds from some tall bushes and watched them as they scattered, took flight into the air and, one by one, lit on the twigs of the bushes ahead of him. Then a movement at his feet. He saw a small cottontail as it leapt away. A little way farther, he passed a lizard sunning itself on a rock. It didn't move when he bent down for a closer look. When he moved on, grasshoppers took off in various directions into the brush, and a white butterfly rose in front of him. A hive of activity around him. All their ancestors, too, it occurred to him, must have been part of the parade—all down through the centuries.

He came to a patch of ground near the cliff, covered mostly with tumbleweed and a reddish ground cover, a pole fence enclosing a square of ground that held a gravesite. On the right side was a tombstone with a plaque encased in a frame of bricks that could have come from one of the dwellings. *Richard Wetherill,* he read, *Died, June 22nd, 1910.* A century ago. On the other side was a chunk of rock: *Marietta Wetherill,* he read, a metal plaque recording the dates of husband and wife. At her headstone was a bouquet of yellow flowers. The site appeared to hold other graves, unmarked.

Richard. The one I was with, lost in the blizzard. That was the beginning. Here his path ended. His fate. The woman was left to wander. But now they're both home.

So they had spoken, and their voices hung in the air: *I want to be buried right up there next to that big, round rock near the cliff. . . . I'll be buried there, too.*

The explorers. Richard. He and Marietta—they lay there, part of this place forever.

Hawkins could see them. The man was lean, brown hair combed back from an irregular receding hairline, a weathered face with a ragged mustache over a firm mouth. Determined, undaunted. The eyes looked beyond Hawkins, as though they would always be gazing into a buried life, a vanished civilization. The air seemed to pulse with what the man had carried. Here was one who'd been seized by fascination. How powerful a force it was. From that first thrill of discovery, fascination had snared him and would never let go—the passion to discover, explore and preserve a vanished world.

But that wasn't all. Hawkins could hear music, lively music, leading him into a room where there were dancers. Richard was standing at the side, watching a young girl, hair curled back from a soft face with a high forehead, large dark eyes that looked around with interest and curiosity, a firm mouth that suggested strength: Marietta Palmer, plump, womanly, smiling as she played her guitar or laughing as she danced, filled with merriment. Richard's eyes were on her, but he couldn't join in— he did not know how to dance. He knew how to work cattle and run a ranch, but he was slow to speak. Even so, the young girl claimed him.

Hawkins saw them out in the rough land, where she seemed to relish adventure. She narrowly missed being crushed by a falling rock. And what led up to Richard's proposal of marriage could have taken her life— crossing the San Juan River in the swiftest channel of its current, wagon and mules being carried downstream. She was holding onto the seat of the wagon, holding on to save her life.

Were you frightened? Richard asked her, when they were safely ashore.

Of course I was. I was scared to death.

Hawkins had to marvel at her—she could do that. She'd gambled on Richard to take her to safety—she'd gotten past fear to do it. They'd both won.

Tell me, what do you do with your fear?

Well, I just swallow it. I couldn't say a word.

Speechless with fear. He knew about that. It had enveloped him like a cocoon, taken over his life so that he couldn't continue. Still it hung over him. But she'd managed to get past it.

Then the culmination of their time together, their respect and admiration for each other: *Will you marry me?*

He was twice her age. *I will have to think about it.*

But he was a man determined in this as in everything else. *I think we were meant to live our lives together. I'll do everything to make you happy.*

Another gamble, about where she was going to put her life. *Well then, I will marry you.*

Hawkins watched them, brought by fascination, arriving to settle there in Chaco Canyon, not far from where he stood, camping under the cliffs at Pueblo Bonito, choosing a site for their house, where first they determined to build a trading post. Cramped up in one room to start with. He watched as they added a room that became bedroom, living room and kitchen, a long narrow room with a bench running along the walls, and windows set in stone masonry. Then others.

The trading post, where the Indians came to buy coffee and sugar, flour and calico, to trade their blankets and silver work. Obstacles rose in the path, and Richard tried one thing after another to stay afloat—the trading post, setting up the Navajo women to weave and sell better blankets, raising sheep, and putting them out to the Navajos on shares. Gambling on one thing after another, trying to take control—to clear the stage for what he really wanted to do.

Hawkins stood lost in what was shaping this man's life—a reel unwinding before him—creating the path Richard would follow to the end. His mistress, who had emerged out of the mystery of things, for him to serve. As though she were, if not all that mattered, the underlying impulse of Richard's life. Nothing would equal the excitement as that other world broke into the ordinary—the way the hairs stood up on his skin and a tremor seized his body when he opened up what had lain hidden.

Hawkins was seized with a sudden envy towards the figure before his eyes who had spent his life looking into the secrets of the past. Was it like getting high, getting drunk and staying that way? Hawkins couldn't imagine anything else. He could imagine Wetherill now as he went from room to room of Pueblo Bonito, carefully excavating, measuring, making notes.

His Navajo workers called him by the name of the ancients, Anasazi.. He somehow attracted them to his cause with the wage of fifty cents a day, despite their terror of any place that harbored death. Somehow they were there digging up the burials of the ancient dead, against all their taboos, against their fears. Days upon days of digging, finding little or nothing, working with patience, but then here, the unimaginable: a hundred of the cylindrical black and white pots, all sorts of bowls and jar covers! More and more in this rich find—turquoise, dozens of pieces of jewelry. A hoard of arrows, a bird effigy inlaid with turquoise.

Come and see, Marietta. It's unbelievable.

Fred will be so pleased—you'll have to write.

But first the work. Everything to be numbered, measured.

And look here. Anasazi picked it up from among the pieces of jet—

Why it's a toad with a turquoise in its head.

Looks more like a frog.

You think they traded it up here?

I think there was water here once. It'd dried out considerable.

What did it mean, a lowly toad or maybe frog with a jewel in its head? What had made it so special? There were the questions that lingered after discovery, part of the fascination. Hawkins was momentarily dazzled into forgetfulness of where he stood.

The children came—they were a family. Five kids, four that lived and grew to adulthood. Marietta had a life with them, nursing and feeding, tending to their play and education, their dogs and horses, their love of being out-of-doors. She and the kids liked to sleep outdoors, she always liked that. The panorama of their lives opened out before him. Hawkins saw her at her tasks, washing and cooking for the men after a long day of work, caring for her children, riding her horse out to distant hogans to visit.

Now Hawkins was among the many visitors who came, and she was seeing that they were well fed and had what they needed. Wife, mother, hostess, nurse, archaeologist, and musician, who carried her music with her.

I never wanted to live anywhere else. Only here under the buttes. For her eyes were turned to the present— She had her passion as well: the inhabitants of the land. *I lived among the Navajos and learned their language.. I came to know them—they trusted me. They told me their stories.*

Near her stood one of the Navajos, a gray-haired old man, whose face seemed to carry a sense of tragedy. No doubt his memory went a perilous way back, to the Long Walk, when Kit Carson rounded up the Dine and marched them to Fort Sumner. Went back to the spirits of all those who had died on that long march in the cold. Perhaps his face had been shaped by the thought of what had happened to his people. *I adopted her as my daughter. Her tongue is thin enough to speak the language of the Dine. She will tell our story to the white man.*

I was admitted to their ceremonies, and oh, to one that has been engraved in my memory ever since. The death of a holy man, who had lost his powers. A terrible death

Hawkins could see how she moved among the people, nursing them when they were sick and helping the women with childbearing. Her life interwoven with theirs.

Two worlds had come together for the sake of another, there for the sake of discovery. *And this is something new—something different from* the Cliff Dwellers. Richard stood holding an intricately woven basket, taken from the head of one of the skeletons the workers had unearthed. Once again his heart was given the chance to leap with joy at what had been uncovered. How many discoveries had come from delving deep and working back? Back to a tribe of people different from the others. *Look at this—these people had baskets—there are no pottery shards. They didn't have any. They lived in these caves before the Anasazi came. I'm sure of it.*

These were the Basket Makers, their world merging into the next, that of the Blue Cross people and the Cliff Dwellers. Who knew how many tribes had wandered through and put their marks on the walls of the cliffs before the doors of the pueblos were sealed shut and the Canyon abandoned. To be followed by the Navajos who lived on the land, and the various tribes, Hopi, Laguna, Zia, Zuni, who traced their ancestry here. And the Wetherills and their descendant—all were part of it.

It was a story now, waiting to be told to all those descendants who came to the Canyon and learned the names of the ones who'd come before. A story. What Hawkins could see unreeling before his eyes, and what he would come to know. All swept up in the whirlpool of a single large fact. A man lying on the ground, murdered: his blood on the land, the sound of gunshots in the air. And in the air, the cries of a woman and her children. Hawkins trembled for something he did not yet understand and for what lay below the surface.

Above him, along the side of the cliff, the crows rose and flapped their wings, trailing dark shadows on the ground. They dived and cawed, as though presenting themselves at the edge of his mind with something wordless and full of torment. A great weakness overcame him. *Come now, you have the beginning*, the voice told him, *The crows will tell you the rest of the story—what the keenest eyes are able to see, the keenest ears are able to hear.*

IV

After he left the burial ground, he wandered down aimlessly among the cottonwoods along the wash. He was at loose ends, waiting for something. What had arisen at the cemetery unnerved him. It was uncanny, yet somehow real—the lives he'd brushed up against, presences that had now vanished, yet belonged to the Canyon. He didn't know what to make of them, what any of it had to do with him.

The day was still brilliant with sun, slow-moving clouds over the buttes. He was walking among chunks and branches of dead wood from the scrub cedar, cottonwoods and greasewood that grew in the canyon. It occurred to him that he could gather some of the sounder pieces for his fire. The little bundle the Camp Host had given him was almost gone. He hadn't expected to be there this long. He was lightheaded from lack of food. He didn't know how long he had to remain in his present state before he could accomplish his task and be released from whatever obligation he had taken on. What he'd do afterwards still lay in the balance. It was as though he had to wait for some word or sign.

A slight wind had picked up. Though the morning had let go of the frost and there was a golden light and the warmth of the sun would last only a brief while. He would soak it up while it lasted. The Camp Host had perhaps forgotten about him, or else chose to ignore him, figuring that he'd be leaving once the wood ran out. Surely he came around to check the camp sites. The campground still had visitors, mostly in campers and r.v.s—people who did not have to expose themselves to the weather or put their bones to the ground. Some few hardy souls put up tents and cooked their meals out of doors.

He piled the wood in the truck and drove back to the campground. Just as he returned to the site, his neighbor, the gray haired man he'd seen previously, came over, followed by the smell of meat cooking on the grill. "We're leaving early in the morning," he said, "We've got some extra wood if you want it."

Hawkins accepted it gratefully. Better stuff than what he'd gathered. "Where I come from," his neighbor told him, "you hope to find wood when you come to a camp site and try to leave some for the next guy."

The fire would feel good. Hawkins had enough wood to keep it going as long as he wanted to sit by it before he turned in. He'd still have wood left over if he needed it.

It was early yet. While he still had the light, he took his things from the truck, set up his mat and unrolled his sleeping bag again behind the ancient dwelling. He went to the truck for his tarp, unfolded it partway and set it not far from the fire pit. He had no trouble this time getting the wood to catch after the paper and kindling burned. He could sit down and appreciate its warmth, take charge of it and feed it carefully. He was grateful for it, as those who'd lived in the little house must have been, cooking their food, warming their bodies against the desert cold. The smell of food teased his appetite, made his stomach growl. He thought of how it would be to take a freshly killed bird or rabbit in its rawness and blood and putting the fire to it, what it mean to cook something, how it invited you toward a sense of the warmth and the comfort of home. He wasn't sure what home meant for him anymore. Ruthie had provided one in her haphazard way. He'd had a few glimpses of others here and there, but they were strung together by disjointed moves from here to there.

As his eyes followed the leap of flames, he found himself drifting away from his surroundings—the mountains deepening to indigo, the shadows that played on the cliff behind him, the lingering afterglow of the sunset on the clouds. Drifting once again toward the strangeness that had met him there.

A strange place, Chaco Canyon. He felt intensely alone in its vastness, and a conflicted sense of his being alive, being the confused bundle of emotions that had led him there, sitting in the center of what now lay in the past. His past, as part of a larger past he knew nothing of. That past was filled with things lost, maybe found again but with living flesh stripped away. Only bits and pieces left, part of a broken puzzle. You dug them out. Or maybe something came to you in the middle of the night you might not even want. Just now, the voice had left him alone—he would almost have been glad for its company. He wasn't done with it yet—he was quite certain of that. Or the Wetherills. There was more coming.

In spite of himself, curiosity had hold of him. Crows would bring him the rest of the story? He couldn't feature it. Birds that came with death, flew around looking for it—that bothered him. They'd be coming for him, too, after he . . . He couldn't think any farther.

The warmth of the fire was making him drowsy, the wood having burned down to glowing coals. He could feel the chill settling in, but didn't want to move even though the ground was hard under him. He pushed himself up and went off to the men's room, to use the toilet and wash up, then came back, folded up the tarp, and moved to his little dwelling under the cliff.

He got comfortable in his sleeping bag and lay there taking in the smell of earth and old adobe. A certain comfort resided in what was solidly around him, something ancient that lay in the smell of the stones and grasses. He heard a rustle from some small bit of life sheltering. Then he heard a sound like a moan, perhaps the wind stirring. He wanted just to let go, but the sound came again, troubling him, a human sound.

I'm not going to be beaten up anymore by that drunken bully. A voice— this time a woman's voice. It called up what he had heard long ago, when the words had pulled him out of sleep. He was lying there under the covers while, in the upper bunk, Clyde whimpered but didn't wake. Alone in the dark, he was holding onto something soft, clinging to it. A bear, the furry yellow bear he slept with every night, who whispered to him stories about the other animals that lived in the forest.

He was lying there again with the sense of the bear beside him. But then, half-awake, he had no idea what had happened to the bear.

He felt a sudden anger. How had it disappeared? It seemed terribly important for him to know. A keen sense of loss came over him. He rolled over and tried to push away what he was hearing.

Get out while you can. Go someplace where he can't find you Ruthie's voice, hoarse from smoking.

The other voice he wasn't sure of at first, hearing it from down the years. Familiar, but so changed, so choked, It was almost a sob. Piercing him. *There's no money—he hit me, took it all from my purse. Probably drunk it up by now.*

I'll give you money. Get yourself together, leave the boys with me till you get settled. Get away while the getting's good.

The two voices met in such urgency he could hardly breathe.

Do it tomorrow. You're young—you've got looks and talent. You can have a better life, Annie.

The fear came back even now, like a stone that weighed on his chest and knotted his innards, made him want to throw up. As Hawkins lay there now he could hear every sound the night had to offer. An owl hooting in the distance, the wind shifting, the clicking of branches. He lifted up on his elbow and looked out through the window space. It was very dark outside, cloudy, but with a few spaces with stars.

It'll be all right. I've just got to hang on a little longer, till I've got enough cash. He'll sober up for a few days. Booze is a demon inside him.

No, don't wait—here take this and just go. I'll keep the boys. I don't trust him.

They were trying to distract him, two women he didn't know. *Here's the church and here's the steeple . . . open the doors.* That came back to him. People inside. Someone sobbing. A small boy holding Ruthie's hand on one side, Clyde on the other, both of them dressed in their little dark outfits. Something bad had happened. He couldn't stop crying. And he kept it up till they got back to Ruthie's trailer and Clyde yelled at him to shut up. But he couldn't.

Clyde dragged him out in front of the trailer, then hunted around in the weeds till he caught a grasshopper. He squeezed it until it made a yellow spot in his palm. Then he crushed it. "See, it's dead." And he howled till Ruthie came out, whacked Clyde once across the head, then cradled both of them in her arms. He couldn't understand why his mother wouldn't come back. He couldn't understand *accident*.

He was not quite four, and Clyde was going on eight when they came to live with Ruthie in her trailer. He looked around as if he were set down in a strange world and didn't know how to speak the language. He didn't want anyone to touch him. He shrank back from other kids. And when he was old enough to go to school, he cried when Ruthie left him there. He stood apart. Ruthie tried to get him to play with Jimmy across the street, but he preferred to sit with a picture book or blocks or toy cars.

Loud-talking, cigarette-smoking, beer-drinking Ruthie—she had taken over and did what was needed. He was there trying to go along, not knowing what he was supposed to do unless she told him. She cooked their meals and left food for them when she had to work late. Clyde was the one she depended on. He did what he was told. Hawkins was another kettle of fish. He left clothes scattered on the floor; he was a picky eater and played with his food till he drove her nuts. He was afraid of the dark and woke in the middle of the night. He had to be scolded into doing his homework.

He and Clyde didn't get along, though Clyde did look after him. Once when a fourth-grader started to bully him, Clyde went after his tomenter and beat him up. Nobody bothered him after that. The nights Ruthie had to work and put Clyde in charge, they were both on their good behavior, though Clyde called him "twirp" and tried to boss him around. They watched t.v. together, and played checkers. Sometimes Clyde helped with his spelling and arithmetic.

Clyde knew things he didn't know, but wouldn't reveal them. At times when he was older, he tried to ask about their mother and the accident, but Clyde wouldn't talk. Once Clyde said out of the blue, "I know where our dad is, and you don't." Hawkins tried to beat him to make him tell, but Clyde was the stronger and left him with a bloody nose.

Ruthie was always a riddle Hawkins had no answers for. To him, she was old. *You get to be forty-five, darlin', the men stop lookin'. They want the young chicks.* As he lay there remembering her, Hawkins realized he knew very little about Ruthie's early life—there'd been a man in it He knew only that she'd spent a couple of years being miserable before she got out, took her kid and went her way. She'd dropped out of high school to get married. Never bothered with a divorce.

He could see her in her waitress outfits with a clip to hold back her long glossy hair. She'd worked in bars and cafes around the town. She worked nights so she could be home with him till he was school age. Sometimes she took Hawkins with her, and he could remember sitting with his coloring book or puzzle while she served drinks, kidded and flirted with the men and laughed a lot. At home her mind was usually elsewhere, and he found it hard to read her mood from her expresssion.

She got good tips. And she didn't lack for dates. Men drifted in and out of her life, nothing permanent. He would hear voices as the front door opened the nights she brought some guy home; then action in the bedroom. He always kept quiet, pretending to be asleep. Every once in a while she'd come home early with someone she'd met at the cafe and cook supper for all of them. Sometimes the guy would take them out for a hamburger and play catch with him and Clyde afterwards. But after a few months, they went and didn't come back.

The way Ruthie nailed them made Hawkins think that all men were duds. She told about her women friends about her adventures— with a salesman, a truck driver—mechanics, construction workers, and once a guy from the gas company. She rated them as she and her friends sat around dissecting their sex lives, not knowing or caring about what he took into his head.

"I got all worked up, but he was a dud from the git-go. Had only a couple of drinks in him, but he couldn't get it up. Wanted me to suck him up. What kind of man is that?" Once when she'd been particularly horny, she said, she'd snagged a truck driver and they'd gone to a motel for a little fooling around after she got off work.

"That big oaf. The only thing he has is what he had between his legs. But I got what I wanted out of him. A little present to myself." He'd gone off into a snore afterwards, she told them, and she'd taken a ribbon from her hair and tied it around his big toe with a little tag and a dollar bill. *Thanks for the bang.*

"You ever going to get married again?" her friend Connie asked her. Hawkins was curious to know. She just shrugged.

But maybe that was the shell she put around herself to keep from getting hurt—because there was that one time she fell hard. He knew all about that one. And it was clear afterwards she wasn't going to pick herself up again. This time it was man who'd already been like a father to him.

He was about thirteen at the beginning of it. Ruthie got a letter that put her in a state of nerves for days. Her sister, Lena, was asking for help. Up to that point, Hawkins didn't know she even had a sister. "We've been out of touch," was all she said about her.

She and her husband, Pete, ran a café over in Chama, doing well until she developed an ulcer in her leg and couldn't be on her feet anymore. They had no insurance and their medical bills had just about wiped them out. Could Ruthie come and help out, wait tables, help with the dishwashing cleaning up. She'd have food and a trailer to stay in. Pete did the cooking.

Ruthie didn't agree right away, not even when Lena called and they talked a blue streak. It meant giving up the trailer they were renting, she told Lena, and putting her stuff in storage, pulling the boys out of school, and taking them to a strange place. Her job didn't matter so much. She could get another when she got back, if they weren't willing to take her on again.

"She knows how I feel," Ruthie said, "It's asking a lot of me, especially when we . . . well, it's a long story. I guess it's pretty bad—she's begging me."

Finally, Ruthie gave in. Clyde would be staying behind. He was already working for a ranching family, helping with the stock, exercising their horses, and making himself generally useful. The family had become fond of him. They looked upon him as a son.

They'd see to it he'd get his diploma. They were convinced he had it in him to makesomething of his life and were eager up to give him a boost.

For himself, Hawkins was full of anxiety. School had always been a problem for him, though he wasn't doing badly in junior high. Mrs. Montoya, his history teacher, told him he was smart, and he tried to do well for her because she praised him. It was the only subject he got good grades in. He still didn't hit it off with the other kids. In some ways, he was glad to leave the school and everything else behind, Clyde for sure.

As Ruthie drove her Ford over to Chama, piled with clothes and the household stuff she thought they'd need, he was thinking about what he could do if he got into a fight.

The trip left him wide-eyed as they traveled through the mountains. They'd almost never gone anywhere except out for a picnic now and then. They drove through the little towns, stopped in a rest area to eat sandwiches and have a coke. Along the highway into Chama, he was struck by the fancy-looking motels and restaurants for the tourists to land in after they'd ridden the narrow-gauge railroad up to Silverton. He was keen to do it himself.

When they found their way to Pete & Lena's, he saw that the place was made out of a trailer. Nothing fancy. He found it odd to see the wooden figure of an Indian woman standing beside the door. A sign, planted in between an American flag on one side, and a flower-covered welcome flag on the other, insisted they step right in. When they did, they found various customers sitting at the formica tables with their beers or coffee in front of them, relaxing in the space between lunch and supper. Some were high school students. There to welcome Ruthie and him was his uncle Pete.

"Hey there, Hawk, give us a hug. So good to see you, son—and you, too, Ruthie—it's been too long."

Ruthie gave him a slow smile and a nod, while Hawkins stood inside his uncle's hug. It was an awkward moment, as if both Ruthie and his uncle were holding themselves in. He liked Pete's face—his smile made a place for him. He gave off a good smell partly from the food he was cooking, chili maybe, and partly from something that belonged to him alone.

A lot went on in a little space, he remembered. He knew every inch of it. How often he'd stood in its midst with the feeling it was the best place he'd ever occupied. A counter divided it, cash register on top, in the company of glass jars filled with cookies, and a shelf of apple, cherry, and cream pies underneath. A small television was mounted above. Behind the counter was the cooking area, nearly everything within reach—a well for doing French fries, a grill, a machine that dispensed soft drinks, a coffee machine, microwave and refrigerator. On the way out or the way in, you could see an old bureau, painted cream color with blue drawers, on the top, a blue vase of artificial morning glories and hydrangeas. For him, it was the prettiest thing around.

The local folks came to eat hamburgers and frybread, burritos, enchiladas with sopapillas and honey, guacamole, menudo, and other Mexican and Indian dishes. While they ate, they there was a running commentary on the weather, sports, the politics of the city council, who was sleeping with whom or getting a divorce, and other items of local interest. Every once in while a passing motorist wandered in, sometimes with a family, all regarded with casual interest.

In a little while, it seemed like he was one of them, without his even thinking about it. The locals greeted him as if he belonged there. In turn, he appreciated all those who came in the door, to appreciate, along with him, the various pieces that made Pete & Lena's Cafe what it was. Inside, the Virgin Mary, who lent her presence to the passing of time. He could see himself sitting on one of the stools gazing at her, wondering what she was doing on a clock—she was so far away from anything that had to do with time. And the Last Supper, framed on the opposite wall, occupied a space far beyond the tables filled with the teenagers eating their burgers and French fries, the girls talking about boys, the boys about basketball and girls. Maybe the main thing was they all had food.

That was *home*, he thought now. The sense of coming there from school and finding family. His aunt and uncle. Pete busy cooking in his space behind the counter, looking up and giving a greeting to those coming in. He moved so fast with the orders, flipping burgers, pulling the enchildas out of the oven, putting together the tacos, Hawkins always wondered how he managed it. Kept him thin. The older women said Pete was a dead ringer for half forgotten movie stars. Pete could always get a laugh out of him. He liked helping out—taking out the trash, sweeping up after the place closed.

On Sundays, he and Lena took him to church, where, if he didn't connect with what was going on, he was still glad to be in their company. Ruthie never went along. "They can have all the Hail Mary's and confessions they want," Ruthie said. "Me—I got my fill of that kind of hogwash—up to here." *Here* was pretty high up.

When he lay in bed just before sleep, he would think of Pete, whisper his name over to himself. As though he couldn't believe the reality of Pete's presence. It was a new experience having a man in his life who treated him a son. "Hi kid," whenever he came into the café. He could hear him now, the warmth of his voice. "How's it going? What did you do today?" He'd give Pete a run-down. There was going to be a basketball game. Would Pete like to go? "Hell, yes, I wouldn't let go of a ballgame, especially when my nephew's in it."

There was a cute girl who sat in front of him, but she was shy and always looked down when he tried to talk to her. "Well," Pete said. "You just keep saying nice things to her, and one of these days, she'll look up and smile, and the two of you can come here for a coke." The way Pete laughed and slapped him on the shoulder . . .

And the two times Pete took him on up into the forest in Colorado. Great occasions—being outdoors, going fishing and tramping through the woods. Just the two of them—frying up the trout when they got back.

He wasn't doing badly in school either. He discovered he liked learning things, especially about animals and birds. And though he hadn't put the thought into words, he could count on things being in place when he woke up in the morning, with a brightness around the day. Something different from the years in Ruthie's trailer when he dragged himself out of bed and dawdled over breakfast before being hustled off to school.

But something was brewing under the surface that troubled him, that he could only sense without understanding it. Not just that Pete and Ruthie enjoyed one another's company—there was something beyond the way they played with each other, joking and making smart cracks and laughing, and the way they'd razz one another if either of them made a mistake on an order. Making such a big deal out of it, going beyond all bounds, almost like they were trying to hurt one another into saying "uncle." Something moved around and between them as they talked about their customers, though they never said anything out of the ordinary. Maybe that was it—underneath what they said they were speaking about something else entirely. And their bodies had a language of their own.

Pete knew everybody. They came in to tell him their troubles and the latest jokes and gossip. "You gave those boys credit?" Ruthie said once.

"Yeah, they came in hungry—you saw the way they wolfed down those hamburgers. They'll pay. Hank's a good kid. Just a little short on cash now and then."

"You'd feed the whole town."

"Probably would."

Old women, Mexican and Anglo, Hawkins watched them go behind the counter, give Pete a hug, ask how Lena was doing and then go back to the trailer to visit with her or take her some jam or soup or cake or a bunch of flowers. She wasn't doing well. In a lot of pain from the ulcer. It refused to heal, perhaps because of her diabetes or some other underlying problem. Medication didn't help much. Her moods—gloomy and anxious, gave way to crying jags. He hated seeing her cry. "How'm I going to get back on my feet and do things right?" she complained. "I hate just sitting here watching the damned boob tube."

Pete always trying to soothe and comfort her, Ruthie, too. Hawkins didn't know what to say. Ruthie did the shopping and brought her meals. He ran errands, bought her favorite magazines,

People, Reader's Digest and *Cosmpolitan,* plus paperbacks to keep her occupied.

Something was in the air. Sometimes Pete looked distracted, his brow furrowed over some knot he couldn't untangle. The joking between him and Ruthie went on, but it had a forced quality; yet often she displayed a tenderness that Hawkins didn't often see. There was a meeting of the eyes, an understanding that was growing beyond words.

Then it was coming at him, the day his world broke apart again and nothing was the same afterward.

As usual, Ruthie had gone over to take Lena her evening meal, and he was coming along not far behind her to bring her a stash of paperbacks, the romances and detective stories that helped her make it through the day when television got boring. Before he reached the trailer, he heard the crash of dishes and tray and Ruthie crying out, "What the fuck!" And the sound of Lena's wailing.

"What the hell is going on? I bring you your supper and you . . . look what you've done. All over my clothes . . . That hurt, dammit!"

"I should have known." He heard Lena sobbing. "Oh, I knew you'd never let go, you'd try to take him away from me no matter what. "

"You're out of your mind."

He was stopped in his tracks. He couldn't go in there. Just turned and ran back to Pete. The café was full of people, orders piling up. And Pete wondering what had happened to Ruthie. Maybe Pete should be there, but then again maybe he shouldn't. Caught in hesitations, Hawkins could only stand there. His face must have told Pete something.

He remembered running back to the trailer.

"Don't lie to me."

A mixture and accusations and cuss words hit the air, he stranding paralyzed.

"You're a big fat liar."

"Okay, tell me what we've done that's so terrible."

"I don't have to tell you. The way you suckered him in. Putting your arms around him. Smooching up to him."

Yelling, knocking at the door, "Pete's waiting on you, Ruthie."

Ruthie throwing open the door. "Get along with you now. I'll be there in a minute. And shut the damned door." He could hear Lena crying and coughing, choking. He just standing there outside, again uncertain and at the same time caught in the desperation to know.

"There's always talk," Ruthie was saying. "It's that bitch, Vicki—I know it is. Just panting for some piece of gossip to blow up into a shitload of trouble. Just loves it. She's had her eye on me from the beginning.

"What d'you know about Vicki?"

"She has an influence on you—a bad influence. I can see right through her. Are you going to believe Vicki over me? Are you going to do that?"

"She's a *friend*," Lena shrieked . "A good friend. She looks out for me."

"As if I don't . . . Your sister. And look how you treat me."

"I just knew in my bones I couldn't trust you around Pete."

A long silence. Then in a quiet voice Hawkins could barely make out, a change of tactics. "C'mon, baby, I know you're hurting. But don't throw oil on the water. Pete and me, we've had a little fun with each other—that's all. You can't blame me for that. You know what happened in the past, and besides that, we came from people who can let things go off the trail for a little while and not cause any harm. And if it happened once or twice it wasn't taking anything away from you. Just trying to make each other happy. We all love each other, you know that. "

"Oh, so now you admit it. Just putting me off, trying to honey me out of it. I don't care what happened between us. The past is over, and this is right now. And you know as well as I do our family left the rez a long time ago, a way long time. They went into the big world, married other people, white, Mexican. We don't go the Red Path anymore. Since when have you been traditional in anything? Hypocrite. Whore. And me a sick woman—you'd do that, you . . .

"You got it wrong," Ruthie said. "Why can't women give themselves to men they like without having it thrown in their face?

You're trying to hold onto something that isn't there. When what we've got is precious and wonderful. There's love. Pete loves you and he loves me. We're all in this together. And I love you both, I really do."

"Get out, just get the hell out."

"Listen," Ruthie said hoarsely, "you broke my life in two. Who gives you the call—just sitting there being waited on . . . I'm trying not to hate you."

There she came clattering out of the trailer. Hawkins ducked away just in time to dodge off. Pete was coming now, and he and Ruthie met on the way out. When he put his hand out to touch her, she shrugged him off and didn't say a word, just headed back into the café.

Hawkins didn't know what further words were spoken between any of them, but the next day Ruthie, sober and silent, started collecting her stuff, and Pete, just as silent, helped her pack it in the car. Though he knew better, Hawkins was whining like a little kid. "Why are we leaving? Why do we have to go?" School wasn't out yet. He had to leave behind his buddies, his teachers. And Pete. Didn't even have a chance to say goodbye.

"We're leaving because we're not wanted here anymore," Ruthie told him stonily. "No more questions, okay. I got a shitload of stuff to do."

The drive back to Farmington was as heavy as grief. A night in a motel. The next day finding a trailer to rent. Ruthie got her old job back in the bar, and he was back in school, still in junior high. He was lying there now trying to put it all together. The kids he'd known kept their distance. They'd made their own alliances without him, and he wasn't about to be taken into them. The town looked different to him, a place he'd stepped out of. Even the air felt different. He had felt oddly separated from his life. He couldn't wait till school was out.

It didn't matter to him when the letter came from Pete that Lena had died. It had all been over for him long before.

V.

The crows will tell you the rest of the story. They saw how it would all unfold, how the end lay in the beginning, and they watched all the strands come together with a single spinning center like a spider's web. Go back and listen to the crows.

The voice had come into his dreaming, and Hawkins woke with a sense of urgency. *Hurry now before they begin their hunting.* He washed up quickly, stowed his sleeping bag and flashlight, then drove back to the parking lot at Pueblo Bonito. Once again, he walked to the gravesite. He looked for the cottontail rabbit he had seen the first time he came there, but it was early, and it had not ventured forth. Nor did any lizards cross his path. Only the crows awaited him, occupying the shelves of rock along the cliff near the gravesite as though they permanently claimed the spot. A few stragglers were still settling themselves. Their wings rustled as they rose and flew back and forth over the butte.

The brightness that had heralded the morning seemed to diminish and the sky to darken as taking color from the crows' wings.

What should he do? Hawkins looked around in confusion, not yet attuned to the day or what the day might demand of him. The day itself seemed shadowy.

First gather some sage and place it on the rock in front of you, the voice told him. *Then light it so that the smoke rises. The elders will come.*

But why? he wondered. What could he get from crows?

He gathered the sage and after some effort, managed to get it to ignite and smolder. The smoke wafted upward and dispersed, leaving its pungent odor. As he stood waiting, he seemed to move into a darkness. The crows seemed to gather to themselves. Even the violet sheen of their wings was darkened. Their cawing, the beating of their wings filled him with disquiet, a sense of alarm. To steady himself, he leaned against a shelf of rock. Where had the sun gone? He saw that the crows were descending and landing on different ledges along the cliff, some in little clusters.

Steady now, the voice told him. *Hold strong.*

Shots rang out, and a man fell to the ground, a bloody wound in his chest An Indian leaned down over him. *Are you sick, Anasazi?* He shot him again in the head, and drew back in fear.

Hawkins cried out in horror. His heart beat wildly, and he put his hands in front of his eyes to shut out the vision. "Oh, what am I seeing?" he cried. "Why have you brought me here?"

You are seeing what brought Richard to this grave. His fate—the end that lay in the beginning.

"And you saw all this?"

I was off at boarding school learning how to be a white man. The government found where Richard hid me, trying to save me from them, and I was taken away. Everything I knew came after. I knew only that my father was dead. Richard was all the father I had. My own father gave me to him. Too drunk and sick to keep me. The ground is sown with betrayals, soaked with blood . Look now—

Hawkins lifted his hands from his eyes and watched one of the crows, its wings rusty as old iron, perhaps from age. It flew from the ledge over to a boulder and landed just in front of Hawkins, cocked an eye, studied him a moment and spoke:

"Behold the crows. We stole the sun from the outer dark and gave it to the earth. We protected men and tried to teach them the right way to live. We rise to seek the light in order to bring our gifts below. We visit this place because all it holds is sacred; we seek to assuage the blood from the past that still soaks the ground."

A sound like murmuring moved among the crows, now settled on the ledges.

"We know the story from our ancestors, from what they saw here, what they heard spoken, and what they knew from the world beyond. It is all that can be done with a terrible story—to save it from being buried and totally forgotten."

By bringing the horror before his eyes? What business was it of his?

"They tried to give warning on that ill-fated day," the crow went on. "They flew around and back and forth over the house, giving their cries, trying to warn those within—a mother and children, and men outside, hands working the cattle. Warning them of the threat in the air." He paused, settled his feathers, then looked up, first to those on the ledges, then to Hawkins. He raised his head and intoned:

"Let me speak, Great Crow, of the man, Anasazi as he was called, lying there on the ground, with a bullet in his head, the man who was killed by another in his rage for what he thought was justice and who brought sorrow to that man, to his widow and children, and to himself—to Indian and white man alike. Tell me then, what is the beginning and the end, for the end lies in the beginning. And the man Chischilling Begay bending over, saying "Are you sick, Anasazi" and firing another bullet into the head of the dying man, drawing back in fear afterward, was only one part of the story, And tell me, Great Crow, what is the beginning of this sad business?

"Say it begins with a boy, a young Navajo boy out with his father to bring back a horse that had run off. Down by the San Juan River. He told the boy to hide in the bushes while he crossed the river to get the horse. Then here comes a white man, a cowboy, riding down the hill. He sees the boy's father, draws his gun, and shoots him. Then rides off. Shoots him only for being there, shoots him for being an Indian. The boy is Chischilling Begay, watching from the bushes, then running to his father. Dead at his feet.

"But Richard could not know what he was moving toward, lost as he was in the blizzard, trying to see ahead of him through the wind-blown snow. And so they appeared to his startled eyes, the cliff houses of Mesa Verde! He vowed to return and came back to excavate them. Overcome by fascination, taken where his passion led him, he came finally to Chaco Canyon. Help me, Great Crow, for there are many strands. Help me to show how they come together. For if the end is in the beginning, it lies in what brought the two men together, and what followed after.

"Let us say that here is the only place they wanted to be, Richard and Marietta. Over yonder by Pueblo Bonito under the cliffs is where they staked out their territory, to explore the cliff dwellings, and settle here and make a life. They were here to explore, to discover the life that was here long ago.

There was some rustling and shuffling among the crows as a young crow slipped off the ledge, perhaps trying to hear better and made a brief commotion in the air before he was settled again. There was a moment's pause in the effort of the crows to regain their attention. The storyteller paused, as though struck by a new consideration. "Help me to speak the truth," the crow began again, "so that the things that happened won't lie in fragments on the ground like the blood and bone of that man's dying. I do it for the trust given me. I do it for the sake of all those here—man or crow, taking this bit of life from the shadows." He looked again in Hawkins' direction.

There was a rustling in the air of something like encouragement, and Hawkins leaned forward to listen more closely.

"There was already a life here, the storyteller said, spreading his wings to take it in. Not the one that built the dwellings or held their ceremonies in the kivas. A tribe long gone. Other tribes came and went, then the Dine settled here. Following them, the white men. The Dine and the outsider, Indian and white man, and for a while the hearts of both came together to work side by side, excavating the ruins and sharing each other's lives. There were exciting discoveries of pots, arrow heads and ax heads, beads, figures, atlatls. Richard wrote down what was found in all the rooms. He discovered the early people who dwelt here and the tribes of the pueblos who came after. He cared only about the world he brought to light. He entered a doorway— He wanted to give that world to the future. He gave his life to preserve the ruins for the sake of those who would follow. He might as well have been speaking to the wind.

"He expanded his house for the children who came to him and Marietta, built a trading post to bring in food and supplies. The Dine came to the trading post, and Richard carried them through bad times and did not take away their pawn. He kept them on the books when they couldn't pay. He helped the women learn to make better blankets so they could get more money for them.

"But they didn't understand very well what it meant to owe

money. They didn't understand when Richard came to take their cattle in payment. He could be harsh, he could be unfair. So they made their complaint. Misunderstandings arose, small fires in the brush. Some thought he was a gambler trying to get all they possessed and take over their lives. These are things that were spoken. One of the Dine complained that Anasazi, had swindled him out of a piece of pawn. Another said Anasazi had cheated him. Perhaps Richard could not see their resentment or know that Chischilling-Begay was a man filled with rage. He owed a large debt that made him resentful and ate at his heart."

The storyteller was growing hoarse and signaled with his wing in the direction of the ledge. Another of the crows flew down, a sleek younger crow, as the old one took his place on the ledge. He then looked around, taking his time to see if his audience was with him, and cast an eye at Hawkins as if to ask him where he was with the story.

For Hawkins, it was as though a question had been tossed into the air. Certain things had happened and taken hold, left their mark, leaving behind their effects. What Richard was doing, what the Dine felt. And there was Chischilling Begay. A man, who must have been angry since he was a boy and saw the killing. Many pieces of life had come into play. His own life was like that, and it was not clear to Hawkins yet how they came to fall for Richard, or how in his time here they would come together for himself. The stone was still in his pocket. The story held him, he was how it would work out. He nodded to the crow as though inviting him to begin again.

"Our gratitude to our brother, the great storyteller of the crows, to take us this far in our understanding," the crow said, casting his glance to the ledge where the old crow was now perched. "He has left it to me to carry the tale forward. May I be worthy to follow in his footsteps. May I, too, Great Crow, succeed in speaking the truth." He glanced around once more. Shifted to left and right, and began again.

"We see how certain things create bad weather, storms that move in and send us to seek shelter. And there is another kind of weather that humans make around them. There were things Richard did not know," the crow continued, taking up the story. "He made mistakes in the human way—for the two-leggeds are not like crows, even though they fly now on borrowed wings. Crows have the gift of seeing things from a distance before they happen, from the air, from the tops of mountains. They can see into the future. But even humans have some of that—the gift of forethought."

Then maybe you can *know*, Hawkins thought, with a sinking sense that he hardly knew how his life had gotten him where he was. How blind were his actions. Never looking behind to see what things were happening in the dark, never thinking forward to how they might leave his path strewn with garbage.

"Yes, mistakes," the crow continued. "He told the sheriff he could run his cattle on the north mesa, when he'd already told the Navajos they could run their own cattle there. Without consulting them. Assured them the grass was plentiful and the cattle wouldn't be there long. Richard had his own stock there as well—cattle, horses, eight thousand sheep out on shares. Some of the Navajos were made poor because his stock was competing with theirs. The Navajos felt resentful.

"And did the resentment build with the debts that mounted at the trading post? Chischilling Begay was one of the poorer Indians, with a wife and children. He owned few cattle and very little turquoise or anything else white man or Indian would value. He bought coffee and flour and other goods from Anasazi and watched the debt pile up, as anger smoldered in his chest.

"These things were happening even as Marietta was learning the Navajo language and helping the Dine women birth their children. Everyone was welcome in her home. But when the diphtheria epidemic took so many of the Dine children, all of the Wetherill's, who were kept in quarantine, were spared. And Richard went about burning the hogans where the deaths had been, in order to keep the disease from spreading.

"This was the weather the Dine woke to, the overcast weather that surrounded them, when they entered the trading post and saw

Richard take their cattle in payment for their debts. Some days the weather was heavy and other days milder, for the men worked for Anasazi, helped him in his work, and he paid them well and helped their families.

"But then two men came to Chaco, and they became part of what happened there. The man Shelton, who took charge of the Navajo Agency at Shiprock and the man Stacher, who came to Pueblo Bonito as agent of the Bureau of Indian Affairs. He had his complaints against Anasazi from the beginning. For the Dine came to Anasazi for advice and the settlement of their quarrels instead of to him. The two together began to spread rumors about Anasazi. They wanted to get rid of him.

I don't think Mr. Stacher is a good man . . . Those words were spoken to Marietta. *The Dine say he says bad things about Anasazi. He's jealous because they come to Anasazi instead of to him. A*nd so a new cloud began to form, a black splotchy cloud that put poison into the air. Jealousy, suspicion. The man was puffed up with ambition. He insisted he was going to build a school in the canyon, though Anasazi argued that he didn't want the Navajos coming in with their sheep and horses and stirring up dust over the ruins. And besides, there was not enough water.

"That was when Stacher teamed up with Shelton, who wanted to get Anasazi out of Pueblo Bonito for his own purposes. Rumors began to fly: Anasazi was mistreating the Indians, selling them liquor, cheating them in their trades, stealing their cattle, misusing the land, trying to keep the ruins for himself. These are the ways the two-leggeds create sorrow for themselves. The cloud in the air became darker, and spread over the sky above Pueblo Bonito. You see how darkness spreads. All of these were strands of the web, woven together before the fatal day. And there you see it written on Richard's grave—June 22nd, 1910.

"But there are other strands to be woven in. One of the Dine, Nez-Begay, had taken a black thoroughbred colt that Richard had given to his daughter Elizabeth, a pet she loved. And the man had beaten it brutally and ridden it near to death. Another of the Indians saw it and told it to Anasazi. And the hand, Bill Finn, the one the

Dine called "Blues Eyes" went the next day to bring back the colt. The Dine had bad feelings about Blue Eyes because he treated them harshly when he went to collect debts. He found the colt in a bad way, head hanging, all in a sweat. He knew it was gone. Nez-Begay came out of his hogan and sharp words passed between them. 'The Navajos are mad,' he said, and grabbed the bridle of Finn's horse, which started to rear. Then Finn hit Nez-Begay on the head with his six-shooter and knocked him to the ground. There Finn left him— he would live. He had to leave the colt to die."

The crow allowed them to imagine the quarrel and the dying colt.

"Chis-chilling-Begay was in that hogan, the brother-in-law of Nez-Begay. All worked up, about many things perhaps, he had gone that morning to Blake's trading post to buy bullets for his gun. 'I'm going to kill Anasazi,' he told the trader. 'What kind of talk is that?' the trader, Blakem said, brushing it off. He went ahead and sold him bullets for his rifle, for he didn't take the man seriously. Chis-chilling-Begay was a man none of the Dine took seriously. He had never done anything to make men take notice.

"Now new anger lay over the old. Anger that had flared up and spread. Among the Navajos that gathered that day around Chis-chilling-Begay and Nez-Begay, a great anger had built and bound them together. When Anasazi came up to them, he told them he would settle the quarrel later, he did not know what he was looking at, what was behind the eyes of those men. He was on his way to help collect the strays of Sheriff Talle's herd being driven to the north mesa to fatten.

"And so Anasazi returned from his errand. The hand, Will Flinn, the man who had struck Nez-Begay with his gun and left him unconscious on the ground, was with him. When they were passing through the draw, the sun was full in their eyes, the setting sun, and they could see nothing ahead of them. Nor did they expect anything. But Chis-chilling-Begay and the other men were waiting. Shots rang out. One struck Richard in the hand he held up and went at an angle into his heart. He fell to the ground, dead. Chis-chilling-Begay rode up, descended from his horse, and bent over the dead man. "Are you sick, Anasazi?" he said, and shot him in the head. Perhaps he thought he had avenged his father. And so Chis-chilling-Begay later said, 'That was why I killed Anasazi—he was a white man.'"

The storyteller had finished his tale. The crow stood still for a moment, then flew to a post of the gravesite, where he looked out on his audience and then flew down the canyon.

Hawkins watched the crows disperse. Some flew to the cottonwoods that followed the line of the wash and others to the top of the mesa. Hawkins did not stir. He could hear the other voices, the weeping of children and the cries of a woman: *Stacher and Shelton have murdered my husband. They're responsible for these Indians and the awful things they told the Indians that caused them to do this. . . ."*

Hawkins was still putting together the pieces of incident, the voices. He was trying to get a picture of how the violence had built, how things had been twisted into hard knots of circumstance and how it ended. But that was not the ending, for Marietta would go on with her five children and face the death of her youngest, Ruth, just one year old, who would die on the day Anasazi was killed.

That is how I lost my father, the voice said. For indeed the loss had been his as well. *I had two fathers and lost them both.*

And years later, as Hawkins would discover, when she told her story for one last time to the man who would record it, her voice broke when she spoke of the death of her Mr. Wetherill. A piece of her life had been buried with him. though she would carry on, a piece of her life had gone missing, buried with her Mr. Wetherill.

And because of his knowing some part of it now, Hawkins would be unable to forget it. It would live inside him, something to be carried forward with all the other stories.

VI.

The day had taken flight with the crows. Hawkins had intended to spend the afternoon climbing the trail to Pueblo Alto, but when he tried to find the stone, it wasn't there. He thought for sure he'd put it in his jacket pocket for safekeeping. After a frustrated search that ate up the time and yielded nothing, he tried to settle his nerves by going for water and filling his bottle. He watched the sunset with its gold-orange-red afterglow that gave a green glow to the sky just above the clouds. It left a burning in him that he couldn't describe. He didn't build a fire, but sat at the picnic table at his site and watched evening deepen and the chill coming on. Then buried himself in his sleeping bag and lay there, wide awake, trying to let go, not wanting to think about anything. He couldn't find a comfortable spot—the ground seemed harder, his body achy. He was nowhere—he was nothing.

Finally, he dropped into a sleep in which he watched himself search for the stone. A sudden movement made him start. He jerked his head in time to see the cottontail that had hopped away from him on the path to the Wetherills' graves trying to escape from him again. His dog, Buddy, gave chase, then sat in front of the rabbit hole waiting for him to come out. Buddy waited a long time, changing his position every now and then. Even after Buddy gave it up, the rabbit didn't appear. Hawkins kept trying to call Buddy away. But when his dog turned toward him, it was a grinning coyote.

He sat up, shaken. He wanted to call Buddy to him and tell him—what? That he was sorry? But the dog had become Coyote, and he couldn't see Buddy at all. He was filled with fear. Then he heard the voice again: *What are you afraid of? Why do you tremble in fear?*

Fear? His stomach was in knots, but he was unable to answer. The question plagued him. The fear that had haunted him for months burned his chest. He'd been so afraid of the unseen hand poised to throttle him, he'd run for his life. Run to the edge of the cliff to find death before it found him. Was he afraid he was still being pursued? He didn't know. But now that everything had been stripped away, and he had been brought to nothing and belonged nowhere, what was he afraid of? He had turned toward death and had drawn back from the edge—something beyond fear had pulled him back. Now Coyote sat in front of him grinning at him, there with his bag of tricks. Not a lean, starving coyote, but a sleek, well-fed beast, ready to dance around him, turn him inside out, dance on his chest and laugh in his face.

And he was lying there, all strung up, trapped in the crazy moment of nothing and nowhere. Tied up in a bundle. "Buddy, come help me," he whimpered softly, and for a second he could see his old companion and felt shame wash over him. Buddy—his friend. *Friend.* Yes.

He could remember. Not long after they came to live with Ruthie, she got him and Clyde a puppy from the Humane Society, a mutt with furry dark hair, a buff-colored face, and dark brown ears, wiggly and eager— She thought it would be good for them to have a pup to play with and take care of. She was smart that way. She thought this one would be the right size for her trailer and their rather cramped living space: "and not grow into some big mutt that would knock everything over."

He remembered Buddy licking his hand. He liked the smell of dog, liked putting his nose into Buddy's fur, liked the way he wriggled and rolled and licked his hand, his face. "Goodness, boy, don't let that dog lick your face like that. He's probably got a zillion germs." He picked him up and carried him around, with half of Buddy hanging out of his arms. Ruthie showed him the right way to hold a puppy, and he carried him around with the excitement of having a live creature in his arms.

For a time, Buddy was more Clyde's dog than his, though Buddy was eager to love both of them. At first Clyde got to feed Buddy, since he was the elder, but Hawkins cried—he wanted to do it, too. Then Clyde put the food in the dish, and Hawkins got to set it on the floor. Sometimes he got to hold the leash when they went for walks. They both took turns sleeping with Buddy at night. But Clyde was a restless sleeper and flailed around at night. Though Buddy might start out with Clyde, after a while, he'd move over to Hawkins' bed and snuggle up.

Animals were more real to him than people. The language of their bodies spoke to him. They didn't need words to express what they were or to create a closeness that nothing else offered. When he put his nose into Buddy's fur, took in the smell of him, he took in a part of Buddy, found the dog in himself. Buddy wagged his welcome—excited, joyful, leaping up on him, licking him, playing with him. Buddy gave himself to him, had taken him on, offering love, and would never betray him. A secret pact connected them. As they grew older, Clyde would go off and play with Eddie and Phil at one of their houses. If they came to Ruthie's place, it was to collect Clyde, take him off somewhere. They didn't come for Hawkins, didn't want him tagging along—he was too little and couldn't run fast.

But there was Buddy. When he came home from school, Buddy was there, waiting for Hawkins to take him for a run. He threw balls and sticks for Buddy and they romped and tumbled together. "Come on in now," Ruthie would call him, "You've got homework to do." "Can't I throw just one more stick?" Always, always just one more.

He liked history, and he liked math; he liked reading stories about heroes and explorers. There was some pleasure in doing schoolwork. "Good boy," Ruthie told him when he finished. "Now I've got to go. There's hamburgers in the oven keeping warm. And buns on the table. I've left out the catsup and mustard, and if you want any beans, they're in the pot on the stove. I told Clyde to get himself home by five." Then she was gone.

He used to like to bounce on the couch cushions when she was gone, and before Clyde got home, and run in the place bouncing a ball—strictly forbidden when Ruthie was home. Clyde took charge as soon as he walked in the door. Mr. Perfect. When Ruthie told them not to do something, he always minded. Hawkins knew he'd tell on him if he found out what he was doing. Buddy would never do that.

They were on their own. Clyde did his homework after supper and the two of them watched t.v. until it was bedtime. Clyde could make popcorn, which Buddy loved. No matter how much you gave him, he'd beg for more. Though Hawkins fell asleep right after they went to bed, chances were he'd hear Ruthie come in, about 1:00 a.m., while Clyde lay sound asleep. Sometimes she'd be accompanied by laughter and he heard exchanges in loud whispers. A man had brought her home and he wouldn't leave for a while. You could hear everything that went on in the trailer, the walls were that thin.

For a long time, Hawkins didn't think anything about what he was hearing, it meant nothing to him—not any of it. Not till Clyde clued him in. "Remember how those dogs came for Jingo?" Clyde said. Dogs from miles around congregated to have a turn when the neighbor's beagle came into heat. Hawkins and he had watched until Ruthie got them to come away. "Come on, you boys," Ruthie said, "You don't have to stand there gawking. You'll have time for all that stuff later on."

But even with Clyde's take on what Ruthie was doing, Hawkins was confused. The dogs were trying to make other dogs, but Ruthie wasn't making children. He let it go, even though he'd been assured that something powerful lay between his legs. At the time, he knew only a single use for it. He saw the word *fuck* on the wall at school, and when he asked Ruthie about it, she told him not to use that word. Somebody with a bad mouth had put it there.

Later, when his hormones were bopping around, and he was filled with embarrassment and confusion about what his body was doing or wanted to do, there was Clyde to keep him informed. He could fathom that he and Buddy shared a common instinct.

Buddy had been part of him even when they moved away to live near his Uncle Pete and Aunt Lena, but when they moved back, things had changed. Then Buddy became just a dog, an animal they had to feed and be given water, to be given attention and taken for walks—a chore. Buddy would come up to him, eager-eyed, begging for his attention. And sometimes he'd go through the motions of rumpling his fur, scratching his ears, greeting him with the familiar words, "Hey old dog, hey pal." But often he'd brush right past, ignoring him, on his way to more important things. Or if he was sitting watching t.v., and Buddy came around, asking for his notice, he'd lay a hand on Buddy's head and give him a little pet or even share his popcorn with him, but his attention was with Bat Man or the most absorbing thriller.

There was something else too. He had changed but Buddy was the same old dog. When Buddy first came, he was little and for a time he'd been open and eager, though something dark lay in the pit of his stomach that he couldn't name. He couldn't think about his mother and what had happened to her, though the things he couldn't understand or take in, remained to jab at him under the surface. "I know what happened to our Mama," Clyde had once teased him. "Something bad—like on t.v."

"I don't believe it," Hawkins burst out. Shut up." He put his hands over his ears. He wouldn't listen, not ever. Ruthie made Clyde leave him alone.

His mother was a grasshopper. Whatever happened, it carried a fear he couldn't name that lived in the pit of his stomach. But for a time, he could bury his nose in Buddy's fur, romp with him in the yard and break into laughter at Buddy's antics. And there was a pleasure in the toy cars and trucks he played with Kenny across the street—he had a passion for the cars—and in the trees he climbed to look down from their height and the picnics they went on, and even what some of what he was learning in school.

Till they came back from Chama and everything had changed like the furniture in a familiar room where the light has shifted strangely. In school he couldn't concentrate. The books he was asked to read were just marks on paper. He fell behind. The science and math, the history, the stories they read no longer held any interest for him. At his desk he spent a lot of time drawing dragons and monsters that were continually at war. Sometimes the monsters won, sometimes the dragons. One of the dragons could blow blue fire and sear open the skin of the monsters, which dripped green gore and shrank into black blisters. He invented stories about creatures from outer space and men who battled with them and usually went down to defeat. His dreams were full of their battles.

When questions came at him in class, he turned sullen. "I don't know." When the teachers tried to make an example of him in front of his classmates, he gave back a smirk and a stare that infuriated everybody. What did he care? What were they to him? He had the urge to stick out his tongue, if it hadn't meant a trip to the office. He relished being a discipline problem. He put gum on the seat of the desk chair in the history room and secretly gloated when the teacher sat on it. He'd have been glad to set the whole building on fire and watch it burn to the ground.

He started skipping out. He'd head off down to the river and mess around down there. There were a couple of older guys, Dick Pinnick and Hasty Martin, who'd dropped out and hung around playing pool and drinking beer, trying to decide whether they'd join the army or hitchhike to California to grow marihuana. They called him "Squirt," and gave him cigarettes now and then or a taste of beer. A sort of mascot, when he didn't get on their nerves. From them Hawkins got the smell of experience, and felt its lure.

He got a weekly allowance that covered video games and movies once a week. Ruthie kept cokes and sweets around. He got a little money from walking old Mrs. Cooper's dog, though it gave Buddy fits to find Lucy's smell on him. He had the guys buy cigarettes for him, and a couple of times they gave him a drag from a joint they were smoking. He tried to keep up with them—they got a kick out of him. He was a poor relation.

As it was lying on the couch one day, Ruthie's purse seemed to glow with a special significance, mysterious and compelling. He stood looking at the worn brown leather bag she'd picked up at the thrift shop. A part of her. He studied its creases, its zipper, the cracked shoulder strap that looked like it would break any minute. He tried to remember what he'd seen come out of it. Lipstick, a comb, a little mirror, and a wallet. And how much was in that wallet? While she was busy in the bathroom getting ready for work, he quickly unzipped the purse, took out the wallet and opened it. A twenty, a ten, and several ones. He slipped out a couple of ones, zipped the thing up and went out on the porch. Buddy, who'd sat watching him, followed him out.

His heart was pounding, and as he ate supper that night, it seemed to him Ruthie was looking right through him. Two dollars made very little difference in terms of the things that kept inviting him to spend money. He wanted to get high like Dick and Hasty did. "You want a snort," they'd ask him now and then. Laughed when he coughed as he tried to smoke it. They had a source. He kicked in a ten spot. Without her knowledge Ruthie got to buy half of his pleasure.

When the school notified Ruthie about his absences, she made his ears burn. "You trying to turn into some worthless mess? You're doing a good job of it. You think somebody's going to pay your way all your life? Not me, boy. You can count on it." She blew out the smoke from her cigarette in a thick short burst. "You listen to me, dammit. You see what my life's like. You need schooling—you need to stand on your feet. I'm not going to be around here forever."

He sat tongue-tied in the office, while Ruthie and the principal settled on his fate. He was to be grounded for a month, and he had to spend two hours a night on his homework to bring up his grades. Clyde, who was doing well in high school, told him he was a shithead. "You start messing up your life now . . ." He jerked his arm in Hawkins' direction as though he were brushing off a fly.

In high school Hawkins discovered different ways to get attention. Much to Ruthie's dismay, he came home one afternoon with a rattlesnake tattooed on his upper arm. He did it to shock her, but her reaction was not quite what he expected. "You threw your money away on that? And where did you get it, I'd like to know."

Part of it he'd gotten from her purse—it had called him again. It was easier after she'd started drinking heavily. She couldn't keep track of money or him. He'd been taking small amounts here and there, saving it up. And he'd been cutting the lawn for a couple down the street when they needed it done.

"What's some woman going to think when she looks at that— that you're some big fucker or that you're some low-down snake in the grass?" She gave an unpleasant laugh.

That meant he had to have his nose pierced. He had to link up with those who flouted the rules and got high or drunk when they had the chance, got in a little stealing and thumbed their noses at the Joe Blows and the cops and the teachers and preachers. Told them the didn't give a rat turd for all their stupid rules and holier-than-thou-nose-in-the-air shit. *They* had something to say to the world with their spray guns and graffiti and beer cans littering the highway.

And to Ruthie, too, though what he had to say, he had no idea. There was the time he heard her, sober now, coming out into a real hangover, rummaging all through her purse: "I had that money, oh I know I had it. He gave me that fifty. Where could I have lost it? And how'll I pay . . . ? And that medicine—it costs so damn much."

He'd spent most of it, but he sneaked the rest back. She'd had to borrow some from Clyde.

When he came home, Buddy was there to greet him, the same as always. It wouldn't matter where he'd been, what he'd done. At times, he wanted to give Buddy a kick just for that reason. It was Ruthie who ended up taking care of the dog most of the time, for Clyde had a job hauling and would be gone weekends. Sometimes she'd get on him. "Are you going to take that damned dog for a walk or do I have to do it?"

"Gotta go," he'd tell her and was out of the house before she could start yelling at him. He was working part time cutting lawns; he wanted to buy a motorcycle. Speed and the thrill of it had turned his head. A motorcycle—an extension of all his energy and drive that had nowhere to go. If he did end up getting nagged into taking Buddy out, his mind was elsewhere. Watching an animal sniffing at bushes, lifting a leg to mark his territory . . . what a bore. He was sixteen, he was a man; he'd left his childhood behind and Buddy with it.

Then Buddy, an old dog now, got hit by a car. Broken neck. Ruthie wept over him, but Hawkins couldn't feel his death. He was bound to die sometime. They buried him in the back yard. He dug the hole. Ruthie stood there mournfully. "I loved that old dog," she said. She looked at him. "He loved you more than anybody."

He could almost see Buddy, a flickering image on the wall of the overhang. Sometimes he saw him as a dog and sometimes as a man. The eyes of either were questioning. The track of his life came up to the present, and in it were the dark spaces of that moment where Hawkins was caught up in his own violence, the rage lived inside him, a force that broke apart any good sense.

He struck out in various directions, not caring what he did or what harm lay in it. When he looked more closely, he saw in Buddy's eyes a sadness that was for him. The eyes still held their expression, though he'd tossed Buddy aside like an empty beer can. No longer of use to him. Buddy never held it against him. Had Buddy been a man, he'd have done the same.

Hawkins had hidden himself from Buddy for a long time because Buddy could see into him, see what he was becoming. He'd been afraid, even though Buddy would never tell on him. He knew he'd betrayed Buddy.

What are you afraid of? the voice demanded once more.

He knew now his deepest fear. He could see how his actions had been taking a shape, just as Richard's had, that he'd always have to hide, not only from others, but from himself. He had been staggering on, helpless against himself and full of a sense of injury. What he did or didn't had no consequence, held no harm if it wasn't found out. That was all that mattered. He had no idea that what he had chosen with no thought was creating something, giving his life a shape that would follow him like a shadow. That night with Drew and the others had offered him a sight of the edge he was pushing toward. He was at the boundary mark of a barbed wire fence. But right at the edge came a revulsion he didn't know he was capable of, And now he was left with his greatest fear—that he wouldn't be able to go on living without hating himself, that he'd already scuttled the future and landed forever in *nowhere*.

VII.

He had come to know the dimensions of fire, as a necessity for survival. Sustaining him, the heat of his body. Creating a circle of comfort and warmth, the dance of flames that took him up into a kind of dreaming, then held the heat in the dying coals. The coals in front of him still glowing from within the coatings of gray ash, and every now and then a little pop coming from the remaining wood. Though he was yawning now and again, he couldn't let go of the day and the story the crows had revealed. Events that burned in his mind. He was restless with them.

It was getting cold. The sky was deepening to the extent the moon would allow, leaving a soft glow arount it as it moved across the sky. He watched it briefly, then lifted himself up from the picnic bench, took the path back to his refuge, set down the flashlight at the head of his bedding and crawled into the sleeping bag.

The day the crows inhabited, along with the voice that spoke to him, seemed to flow into the darkness, carried by a dark fire as part of the same dream that continued with the same dreamer. Now the images led into a territory of wider margins, full of color, blending one into the other, keeping its edge of fire.

He inhabits a strange land of shifting shapes and perspectives, where men turn into eagles and fly toward a distance that moves into panoramas of mountains and valleys, where bears and mountain lions beckon him toward pools whose surfaces blossom with fire, and birds rise with flaming feathers. They whirl about his head singing of stars and planets, invite him to fly to somewhere beyond.

Entranced, he watches as a young woman cradled by the crescent moon, gives birth to messenger crows and doves and birds with turquoise eyes. Then with growing uneasiness, he watches a young woman give birth after a difficult delivery to the toad bearing the turquoise jewel in its head. She offers it to him, insists that he accept it—it is for him. He puts up his hands to resist. Something threatens from the creature. He waits anxiously for it to speak, to deliver some saving wisdom, but it sits in stony silence, as though waiting instead for him to do exactly what?

He comes to know from watching his dream self that he would no longer experience hunger; he is being fed in a different way. The voice is back with him again. He must only look and listen carefully, He is not to pick anything up or try to take anything back except what comes to his eye and ear.

The white butterfly appears briefly. *I am here,* she whispers to him. *But my time is nearly done. I have escaped the frost till now, but soon I must blend my whiteness with the frost and let my spirit free until spring comes again. My eggs sleep in their cocoons, and new wings will meet the spring.*

He is being asked to acknowledge that things go on no matter what he does or doesn't do. As though being at all is a flick of chance, a small accident in the scheme of things, where he has no sense he belongs at all. The Wetherills have been and are gone. And his presence is no more than the white butterfly's. So why the images that tease and promise for a moment and at other times break all the bounds of sense and leave no answerss. Darkening again even as he breathes. A wind springing up snatched the tumbleweeds from their roots and whipped them across the desert. A tantrum of the wind.

He woke to a sense of struggle, trying to keep his moorings so as not be tossed around like one more tumbleweed. He sat up and looked for the moon, but it had disappeared beyond the cliff, out of reach. A chill went through him, and he lay back down and snuggled in again. The desert was a cold place.

When he finally drifted off to sleep, he was back in a darkness he could recognize—restless and troubled—where he was engaged in a battle between conflicting elements, between sound and impulse as against word and action. The wind was blowing harder. The sand was sucked up with the wind, and the branches of the cottonwoods snapped back and forth below. Everything began to pull loose and gyrate until it was impossible to see. Fear oppressed him as lightning flared. Then in a great swirl of energies, a face emerged—eyes that could see through the distortions of wind and matter; lips that could shape breath and words. Syllables that held meaning. He was conscious of himself in the dark. He did not know what to do with the burden of being awake, yet something impelled him to go forward, though he wanted to turn away. *There is darkness here,* the voice said. *It takes a great will to enter the emptiness of the void. What will you take from this darkness?*

A tremor went through him as the beating of wings confirmed the presence of birds, sailing upward, flying in circles, crows such as he had seen at the gravesite, a new flock of them. As he watched one after another, the birds began to disappear, and he was seeing the faces of women. He was hearing a lament.

You've heard only part of the story, a voice said to him. *The actions of men in the world of time. But there is the world of women, those who must struggle to survive, not just for their own sake. These are the faces of women.*

For the flash of an instant, Hawkins caught both the known and the unknown, a vision of his mother: *I'm not going to be beaten anymore . . .*

Her face, emerging and then fading before his eyes, was young and vibrant. A swatch of glossy black hair fell across her forehead, and her eyes, a startling black, held a blue fire, fierce and loving. Hawkins wanted to cling to her image, but it faded before his eyes, and he saw only the fluttering of bird wings and heard a wail as she departed. *I never wanted to leave you.*

Another figure, the voice, he had heard before, emerged from the darkness and the fluttering wings, her face half-hidden, as she sat at the window unable to sleep, sitting up night after night. Faces of women appeared outside, Navajo women who stole up to speak to her and offer help and comfort: *Are you all right? Are the children all right? Do you have meat to eat?*

They were there, despite orders from Statcher and Shelton not to come. *Now I will tell you what happened to me. For life goes on even while you're crying over the terrible things that happen. The women came to me because they were my friends. I was Dine, after all. I'd saved their lives and saved their babies. I'd taken care of them, given them medicine. I fed them when they were poor and helped them in every way we could.*

Now it was all turned around. That's how things happen in this life. 'You've gotten very poor.' they said, 'You don't eat. You cry too much.'

One night something awakened me. He hadn't been buried yet. He was still on the back porch. I saw him standing in the doorway just like he used to do. It must have been a dream or something I imagined, but he stood right in that doorway with his hands up on the door frame as he always did. He shook his head—he looked sad. 'I'm so sorry to leave you like this,' he said. 'I'm so sorry to leave you with all these children.'

Yes, I was left with them, one of them just a baby and a couple hardly out of diapers, and there was little to keep us. Seventy-four dollars in the bank— that was all. Everybody thought Mr. Wetherill was a rich man—I had no reason to think we had no money. We had the stock. But even the insurance he had he'd borrowed against. He never gave on that we had so little. And Stacher and Shelton were out to ruin us. They forbade the Indians to have anything to do with us.

Hawkins listening saw the land swept by the fires of hatred and betrayal, some of the other dimensions of fire.

The cattle were all scattered. The children went out on their ponies to gather them up. We only gathered about a hundred fifty sheep out of eight thousand. We never did find a single cow, and we had lots of cattle. I guess we gathered fifty out of several hundred horses we owned. White people stole the stock, not the Indians. They were too frightened. And they had no way of knowing who it was who came on the land saying they'd come for our stock.

Hawkins could see the face of a woman still young but whose expressive brown eyes had looked upon nearly everything. Her face was open and without guile, open to whatever came, open to whoever appeared at her door.

The trading post, her house, both were always full of activity. Those who came to trade and gossip, visitors to see the ruins, the men who worked them, the Hyde brothers, who sponsored the excavations, ranchers and neighbors, Richard's brothers, Miss Quick, who taught the children, and the children themselves. And for a while, the Stachers, who were given help and welcome. There were all the good times when the house was full of people. *Oh, there were good times. Feasts and good talk and celebrations. I loved it all. I wouldn't trade my life for anybody else's*

The canyon was home, but everything was swept away like the leaves on the cottonwoods. Hawkins could see how things were—all the turmoil as she fought for what was hers. It was a strong fight against the whole scheme of things, the network of people against her.

Chaco was my home, but I was forced to leave it. I fought for it, fought in court to get what was due to me, but it was a losing battle. I got an injunction against Stacher to stop interfering with the collection of debts. But the judge put it aside.

And so she left for another piece of untamed territory. *It was beautiful there, different from the Canyon. Lots of big trees and a creek below, wild strawberries and raspberries growing there. And lightning storms you wouldn't believe. Why those storms could run those big trees into the ground. The children and I used to sit at the window and watch. It was exciting. Well, I knew all about what nature could do. I didn't have to be afraid.*

In spite of everything that had happened, she found happiness in taking care of her babies until the youngest, Ruth, fell sick of an unknown ailment and despite everything in the world they could do, she died on June 22nd, 1911. Exactly one year after her husband died, she had to confront another death. *I thought I couldn't take it, it was just too much. But I did. I had my other children. Everything comes to me kind of the hard way, don't it?*

No matter what, I had to make a living. I built a house and Will Flinn built up the herd and we sold the cattle. He could be brutal and cruel, but he was loyal—he was with me all those years to take care of the cattle while I took care of the house. We wouldn't have managed without him.

She told how hard it was after he died of the flu. How she went from pillar to post—working at a trading post and in stores. Trying to put food on the table and get the children grown. *After he died of the flu, I went from pillar to post. I worked at a trading post and in stores. So you see that's how it was, trying to put food on the table and get my children grown. I did that—I was never afraid of hard work. I was a gypsy the rest of my life.*

But all that didn't matter. *The one thing I did want was to live long enough to see the world give Mr. Wetherill credit for what he did, how he discovered the Basketmakers and explored two cultures and gave them to the world. I didn't care about myself. I just wanted someone to get it down about what he did and the sort of person he was . . .*

Her voice trailed off into silence. For a time Hawkins drifted in and out of her story, her grief, her struggles. Death had woven in and out of her life. But she had emerged, somehow intact, strong, enduring, able to survive. Her children had a mother.

He began to see how he'd entered fear. It was the climate that had coalesced around him, the great dark cloud of it. His mother came to him, a deer pursued until she fell bleeding. She had been there for a brief space, with two little boys to rescue and raise and no one to come to her and tell her he was sorry about how she'd been betrayed. She'd been left without any money, though Ruthie had urged her to get away. She had only a man who would harm her.

How little he knew of her story, but it had lived under the surface of his life, festering, gnawing at him, and he didn't know how to get free of it. Let her come and unravel for him what she had to tell. She was a mother who left her children. Why had it happened? "Please come back ," he begged her.

Somewhere in the fog of darkness in which he was lying, he sensed a movement, then a shape, and finally a voice: *I did things all wrong,* he heard and felt chills down his spine. *But I was young. When you're young you think you know what you want. You trust the way things appear. He came to me with a good face. Handsome—he could be charming. Oh, we're filled with tales of romance and the man who appears just like in the movies is what you're in love with. Without a clue about what he really is.*

He'd never seen what his father looked like. He pictured him as big and burly, a man who could lift his own weight. He must have been the cock of the walk, used to having his way, making trouble for himself, taking things out on his mother.

He could be mean. We were in the car once, and a cat came along and was crossing the road. He swerved to hit it. 'Why did you do that?' I yelled at him—I couldn't help it. 'Hate cats.' That's what he said, as if that was a reason. 'But it was somebody's pet. It had a collar on it.' 'Come on, don't be a gutless female. They can get another one, if they're dumb enough. The world is full of goddam cats.'

That should have told me something. But I let it go. I didn't know how bad, how crazy he could be. I stood all I could for seven years. When he started in on you boys, I knew I had to get out. I'd wanted to even before Clyde came into the world, but I was proud. Ruthie didn't want me to marry him. She knew better—she said he was no good. 'Don't ruin your chances, babe. You got your life in front of you.' I made her suffer over me.

His mother's voice seemed almost too light for sound, but he could hear her. *I didn't know what to do, and I was afraid. He could be tender on the outside; he could be loving at times, though when he took me it was like he was trying to squeeze the soul out of my body so I'd be just a thing for him to use. And when he drank, a demon possessed him. He struck out at everything. I didn't know that before he began to hurt me. Then he'd be all sorry about it. And we'd make up. He'd even bring me presents, like fancy underwear. It makes me mad to see how I fell for it.*

It helped him a little to hear that—to know that something had risen up in her.

I was glad when babies came, first Clyde, then you. There was a sweetness in the house to make up for the rest, though sometimes I was so bruised, I could barely take care of you. I just wanted to huddle up in bed and cry. I tried to protect myself, dodge around him and run to the neighbors. It got worse; he started drinking more. Sometimes the police came to the bar dragged him off. And when he came back, he was crazier than ever. But you couldn't tell him anything. He'd just want to slap me around and beat me up, drunk or sober. He'd try to back me into a corner—he was strong. I'd plead. I think he liked that. How could I take care of you and Clyde? He'd knock me down and I'd huddle up and put my arms around my head try to protect my head and breasts, Sometimes I'd hear you and Clyde crying, and Clyde would run at him and kick him. And just get shoved aside. I was afraid for you boys. But it was me he wanted to beat on. Till that time he struck Clyde across the face. And then I knew I had to get out.

Hawkins wondered if Clyde remembered. If he did, he never spoke of them, never spoke of their father. He kept himself busy. He had a paper route and earned his own money. He always minded Ruthie, and she depended on him. She sent him to the store on his bicycle and sent him around to pay the bills. She saved postage that way. He did well in school and wanted to go on to college and become an engineer. He was a good athlete and had hopes of a basketball scholarship. But he didn't go.

Suddenly Hawkins knew why. When Ruthie got sick, she had no insurance, and Clyde was the one who took care of her. It must have taken his money to pay off her bills—doctors' bills and hospital bills. He hadn't taken notice.

His mother's voice took on a darker tone. *He knew in his bones I was going to leave him, and he couldn't stand it. He must've told himself I was a bad woman. Some kind of whore. That way I was dirt under his feet. That way he could kill me and think the world was better off.*

I was just sitting there quiet, reading a style magazine when I looked up and there he was coming at me with a knife. My mind just went blank. Then I jerked up, but before I could dodge away, he grabbed me, grabbed me by the hair. 'I saw you with that Mexican, the one with the mustache. How long've you been cheating on me?'

There was a long silence, then her voice fading away. *'I never wanted to leave you.*

It didn't help matters that Ruthie stepped up to take care of him and Clyde. She wasn't his mother. She was just there. She'd been a mother once and had to do it all over again.

One of the crows was flying over him, cawing, making a ruckus: *I did the best I could, I did the best I could, Ruthie.* The voice was harsh enough. *Trouble. Making trouble. Nothing but . . .* Hawkins drew back. Maybe that was the gift, the only gift, his father had given him.

VIII.

He'd given enough thought to women as he came along, hadn't he? They'd always been there one way or another. Different in ways he couldn't fathom, with their mysterious parts and secretions—tears and menstrual blood and breast milk. Scary. They'd been closing in on him. And something more awaited him like a threat, made him want to curl up more tightly in his mummy bag, shut out the voice of the crow that hovered in the background, ready to swoop down on him.. *What do you want?* he cried as he heard his name, as he tried to to turn in the direction of sleep. *What do you want?*

They were bearing down on him, forcing him to think of what they did in the world and whether or not it mattered. No longer there as part of the scenery as they stood behind counters in stores, in the check-out lanes in groceries, in the hospital corridors and dentist's office, and behind desks in schools, taking his money, looking after him, trying to teach him whatever they had in mind for him, trying to knead his resistant dough. He ignored them or if they got in his face, he fought them even in his silences. He paid attention to their faces if they were pretty and to their boobs and butts on the sly. He barely noticed them in the street walking with their men and pushing their tots in strollers. Kids, except for Sarah, didn't interest him. He watched them on t.v.—they were all over the place, singing and acting and showing off their their bodies, suggesting and evoking something that lived in his own and demanded action.

They were always there, nagging at something inside him, puzzling, attracting and repelling him all at once. There were the girls his age he'd been drawn to physically but from whom he shied away, because they also frightened him—they were taking his measure and he would come out a loser. But he'd make himself get out on the dance floor and move around so that he could have a girl dance with him, and could occasionally touch her or take her by the hand, contact making the hairs stand up on his neck. All this so that he could feel he wasn't a total flop, even though he felt clumsy and awkward. In high school, he'd never gone all the way with a girl or even gotten all that far. He sensed that there was something in him girls didn't want to tangle with.

Until he met Aline, he hadn't really thought about what women might offer him in a personal way, that one or another might even care for him. Aline occupied him, entered his dreams, igniting his feelings. She was a new experience. And she did it without trying to impress him or improve him. She was just what she was, living, working, taking care of her kid. Yet she asked something of him, awakened a kind of largesse, gave him a sense that his life was significant. He couldn't think about that anymore. When she kicked him out, he was like the shriveled skin of a balloon that has just been popped

The rest was all fragments, little jagged bits of memory, he kept trying to put like pieces of a puzzle with pieces missing. Always before, he kept trying to get a hold of the woman that stood above his life—the mother who hadn't been there for him, a reality of no substance he could only feel as an absence. A lingering pain in his chest he could hardly bear. She existed beyond any woman he knew, larger than life. Sometimes he'd had tried to evoke what she looked like by saying her name over and over. But nothing real came of it. Her absence was the most real aspect of her brief existence.

He'd been left nosing for scraps. "Weren't there any pictures of her—not even one?"

"I had some once," Ruthie said. "They were in a shoebox—I meant to put them in a picture album one day, but the roof sprang a leak the last place I lived, before you and Clyde came aboard. Damned fucking landlord," she said. "wouldn't fix anything. Kept telling him that roof was going to let in a waterfall. Just ruined everything except the stuff I had sense to put in the closet. I could kick myself."

A second loss. Ruthie was the one way he knew to his mother, and he kept at her. "What was she like as a girl?" It didn't occur to him that it was Ruthie's loss, too.

"Oh, she was just like other kids. Played with her dolls and loved her stuffed animals—she called them *aminals*." She smiled, gave a little laugh, as if she were seeing her again, playing with her toys. "She liked to go out shopping me and have me buy her a T-shirt at the mall. She loved having new things, and she loved going out to eat Chinese food. She had a cat called Willie—it was a girl cat. She came up with the name Wilantha, though where she heard it, I'll never know. Invented it maybe. That cat was special. Smart, too. She had a sweet way with her and—" She looked away and shut down. "Now don't bother me anymore. I got things to do. Go find something to make yourself useful."

One more scrap. A memory picture at least, even if it was only Ruthie's. But something was changing. Now that she was gone he had to think about Ruthie, too, what she'd been. Her rush to get their supper on the table and see they had fresh jeans and shirts to wear to school, plus sandwiches for lunch.. What she did around the edges of her domestic life. All that time, he thought only of what affected him directly. She did try to give them the things they liked to eat, usually hamburgers and hot dogs and his favorite, spaghetti with meatballs. She didn't force him to eat vegetables, though she tried. She bought them toys for Christmas when they were little, whatever her purse could afford, and took them to see Santa. She dressed them pretty well from what she could buy in thrift shops and on special occasions bought them at least one thing that could have been called a luxury. She encouraged them to check out books from the library, though she wasn't much of a reader herself. She went to their school when they had parents' night, and she talked to his teachers when his grades went plummeting.

He could see her in her moods and rampages, her hair going wild, her face savage. She had her moments—ever hunting distractedly for her keys or her wallet or her glasses, at times beside herself, a tempest turned loose. She'd yell at them for nothing out of her frustrations, even at Buddy for getting in her way. "Get that damned dog out of here, before I kill him. Right under my goddam feet—the mutt. What the fucking hell am I going to do now?"

A good time for him and Buddy to escape to the park and let Clyde help her look for whatever she'd lost and help her calm down. He had a good way with her.

But one time he got hold of something more than he expected, when he'd caught Ruthie in a different light. One of those moments when she was relaxed, not in a hurry to go and do, and the lines in her face softened, and he could see a young woman looking through her eyes. She'd been going through one of her drawers and brought out an old scrapbook that hadn't been ruined by the leak and sat with it at the kitchen table with its oilcloth covering, colorful with large red rambunctious flowers, scuffed and scratched by what two boys could do. "I haven't looked at this in ages."

He and Clyde took pulled up chairs on either side of her, ready to look at photos they'd never seen before. Buddy had flopped at Ruthie's feet under the table, as close to them as possible.

"You wanna see what I looked like when I was little?" she said. He and Clyde bent over to look at a little kid of about four, with straight dark hair, holding onto the hand of a corn cob doll that dangled toward the floor. The little girl who had been Ruthie wasn't really smiling, but he could see a small dimple towards her chin. He turned to look for it in her face, perhaps to be sure it was the same person. "Cute little kid, huh?" Ruthie said. "There's a lot of water gone down the arroyo between then and now, some of it pretty muddy, let me tell you."

She talked about how her mama, Consuela, could make the best tamales anybody had ever eaten and how she and her papa used to go fishing and come back with catfish for her mother to fry up. "We'd even have them for breakfast." She sat back as though to catch their flavor. "We had our own land then, and both he and my ma worked it. She put up food for the winter, tomatoes and beans and apples and peaches from our trees. Us girls helped with all that and worked in the garden and weeded and hoed in the fields.

Jake helped take care of the sheep with our dad. We had enough to eat and then some, corn and beans and squash and meat and from thechickens and sheep. We could sell some of the food in the market. She paused for a moment as if to dream over that bounty.

"I used to love riding bareback. I had a way with horses; it was like I could see into their minds. Horse thoughts. I grew up with animals, tame and wild. I never liked being around when they killed chickens or a sheep."

Hawkins saw a different picture of her out on the land. Nothing like what she was when he came to live with her.

"They worked hard on that land. Lovely place—you could look off to the mountains. All capped with snow in the winter. Guardians. The folks built the house there with help from the neighbors. Lena and I shared a room, and Jake slept in the loft just overhead. We'd sit around at night and listen to our dad tell us stories about Coyote and Raven and how the world was created. He told us about the tricks they got into and how they could turn things inside out and upside down. He sure had it right."

"Was he Indian?" Clyde wanted to know.

"He was Indian. But my mama was Mexican—her family came up from Sonora a long time ago. She had her stories too, about Pancho Villa, and a young girl everybody thought was a saint and who stirred up the Indians to fight the government."

"Did they win?" Clyde said.

"No, they couldn't win. Like here."

"Do they still live there?" Hawkins asked.

"They're dead, Stupid" Clyde announced.

"How do you know?—you think you're so smart." Hawkins was ready to punch him one.

"You boys— Can't you give me a moment's peace?"

She closed the scrapbook and pushed back her chair.

"Tell us—tell us more," they begged.

She shook her head as though to shake off what she was remembering. "Things went bad after that. Yes, bad. Be grateful for what you got," she said as they waited for her to go on. "And count it lucky you've got food on the table and a roof over your head. "Anything can happen."

Like drought and debt. Two bad years in a row: the crops were meager, and they lost a number of sheep during the winter. No grass to feed them in the summer, and precious little water. "We had to borrow just to buy feed for the winter. We hardly had enough to get by. Pa got a job as a mechanic part time, and that held us for a little while. The church gave us beans and rice and helped us out that way.

"About that time, though, it looked like something good was happening. Along came a mining company offering leases for mining uranium on the reservation. Money for the lease, royalties on the uranium. Looked like we were rich. And there were jobs, too. Papa got on at the mine. Only they didn't tell us that what the mining would do, how it would ruin the land and poison the water. We found out all right—when animals and people started getting sick and babies were being born with twisted bodies and arms and legs. Papa found he had lung cancer and he had to go for in for treatment. Mama was was doing poorly too. It was the water we had to drink. We couldn't stay there—we moved into town, rented a trailer there. Jake joined the army. Seventeen. Lied about his age. I me so I could care of them, was trying to go to high school and was working as a waitress. Lena and I tried to help out. Take them to the doctor and the hospital and all that. Keep the place clean and see they had food.

Things had gone bad all right. Turned inside out. Maybe Coyote's work. He'd never thought any farther back than Ruthie. His great-grandparents. Indian and Mexican.

"'That was the end of it. You had to work for everything you got even on the reservation. The land wasn't all that good. But it was a paradise compared to what came after. Paradises turned into hell. I still have the lease they gave us somewhere in this box." She laughed "Maybe they'll come back and mine some more. Think I'll get rich someday?" They looked at her. She was quick to set them straight. "The company mined out all the uranium they could get and left ugly pools behind, filled with yellow water. Some of the Dine tried to get the company to come back and clean things up. Good luck with that. I never went back— the land's still poisoned."

"And Jake, what happened to him?" Clyde asked

"Jake went off to the army and got wounded in Iraq. Thought he could get some job training and have a better chance when he got out.. We didn't want him to go. He got wounded over there. Terrible things must have heppened to him. He was never the same."

Now that he thought about it, a lot had gone bad in Ruthie's life. "You think you got things to complain about," she told him once when he was grousing about their little black and white television and why they couldn't have a better one. And when she said once, "I never even finished high school," he wasn't convinced that was a bad thing.

She must have had her hands full all those years when she had fhe two of them underfoot. Work and kids. Chickens in back; a hutch of rabbits. She did have a couple of girlfriends who came over to chew the fat when she had time off, and Hawkins would catch her laughing and joking with them. There were the men, of course, and he'd thought a lot about the guys who came around the dry spells in between. Guys who gave off the breath of beer and cigarettes and spicy food. Sometimes he thought she must be pretty desperate.

Most of the time, he didn't think about her life as something apart, or what she felt or thought or might have wanted. Now that her life was over, the whole circle of it closed, with nothing more to be added or subtracted, he was left with questions What had happened to her along the way to make her who she was? What she was like growing up and what had she wanted for herself? Why was she alone without a man when she could have had one, and how come she and Lena had never spent time together? Had Ruthie gotten pregnant the way Aline did? Had she been married? Had her man left her or had she thrown him out?

She'd been tough for him live with, always yelling at him and trying to get some good out of him, swearing at things that stood in her way. Especially him. All he knew was how he just wanted to lash out, and she was ready to lash back. Clyde seemed actually fond of her, tried to defend her and go out of his way for her. Maybe she'd had to grow cactus thorns just to get by and keep things from spinning out from under her. She'd had a kid to take care of on her own, a daughter she'd lost. And two grandsons to nudge onward to manhood. And maybe it took everything she had just to survive.

Not all mothers survive.

Hawkins was convinced now what he'd sensed then only dimly, that something had happened to her when they'd gone to live near Lena and Pete. The way he saw it, she'd fallen in love, maybe for the first time. It struck him now that she'd been carrying that love from a time before, only she'd kept it down. They'd never gone to visit her sister during the years he and Clyde had been with her. They weren't that far away. It was only when Lena got sick and things became desperate for that they'd come back together. Had there been bad blood between them?

Only maybe they hadn't counted on what was smoldering down among the ashes. And neither she nor Pete had been able to keep it from flaring up.

What he didn't know had made things into a before and after in his own life. Things he hadn't dared ask her about. Things the crows knew, as though they'd always hung in the air and would never disappear, things that were somehow a part of his life even if he didn't know what they were.

IX

*L*ook *at me.* Ruthie's voice came to him out of the stillness, *black shiny feathers, and you see that sheen to them, green and blue. A shining. I'll demonstrate.* She landed for a moment on a rock near him in the gathering daylight. *Would you say a darkness clings to me because I appear in this form? Don't give it another thought. An appearance, that's all.* She rose up, circled above him—crow, but more than bird. He recognized her, but she struck him with an awe that was new to him. *You don't yet know the magic at the heart of things. Black as the womb, but think what's inside. Now tell me why you called me.*

Called her. Had he called her? She was there, right on him, and he had to come up with an answer. "I wanted . . ." He tried to shape the syllables to tell her, but it was too complicated. He wanted to give her due mourning—he wanted to give her better than she'd got from him—he wanted to piece together the puzzle of the past—the weight of things known and unknown. He wanted to start over with himself, with something true and real, because the past was foul on his tongue and in his heart, and he was broken into fragments. Could he make a new beginning—was there any seed to make it from? So he'd been made to look at the scraps from the past. Thus far what did they add up to? Where was he supposed to go from here?

He shrank from facing Ruthie. He could see her only as she was during his last visit, shriveled, skeletal, hardly in the world.

He heard a cackle as she swooped upward. *Shee-ut! You think that's all I was, all I am, that my life shriveled up and became nothing, just a lot of rotten flesh and dust and ashes because I slipped out of my skin?*

She charged past him. *Yeah, you blew it all right. Made such a mess of things, you couldn't see me into the next life. Well the joke's on you, friend.*

The same old Ruthie—he was cheered by her irreverence. Though he wanted to let her know he was sorry, things had gone way beyond that. Somehow he wanted at the same time to laugh, to let laughter fill his being. He was thrown back into confusion. He was being asked to rise to some higher occasion, and he wasn't ready yet. *Sorry* couldn't possibly accommodate the long list of things that stood in his way. No more than it had with Aline. He stood empty as a kettle, no words in him.

For the first time you're not giving me any lip, she said, as she did a graceful curve and hovered over him. *A mighty good sign.*

She had dug at him in the past, but now she was pulling at something in him. He could feel it, not just what had been haunting him, but something waiting to exist. Something that struggled within him. She had secrets to tell, but he wasn't sure that she was ready to spit them out or that he was ready to take them in. She was making his head spin. *Ah, now you come to me,* she taunted him, as she swooped down again with a rush of wings, *wanting something for nothing. A good story to tell the grandchildren. Well, here's news for you. You've got a few things to do. And not just putting in the time, going through the motions. Ah, these wings,* she said, as she circled above him. *There were those Greek fellows that tried them out—I don't blame them.*

He felt in his pocket for the stone.

You're miles away from that. You've barely made a beginning. All he could do was wait. In the commotion of wings that swept back and forth, Ruthie was a whole flock. She was making a large disturbance in the air, but then she always did.

I knew all along you were stealing from my purse, she said. *Times were I was pretty short, had to work for extra hours.*

Another blow in the gut. "Why did you let me get away with it?" He heard himself whining like a kid—as though it was her fault. *I figured you'd just get pissed enough to do something even worse.*

And so he had. He was like gunpowder, ready to be set off by any passing spark.

But it was part of my nature to adapt to what I couldn't change. A few swear words along the way—you heard some. I wasn't going to change you, I knew that. I was going to have to sit by and wait for you to smarten up, if you were ever going to— Maybe take a few knocks on the way. Maybe now you're ready for something different.

"Yes," he agreed, in a low voice.

I'm not about to waste my time with you unless . . ." She landed on a branch of scrub cedar and suddenly he was looking into her face. A face that was both young and old. He could even see something of the child that had been in the scrapbook. But her face held something unearthly as well as familiar. The lines in her forehead had been smoothed out.

"I know," he said. "I'll do anything you ask." He had to look away.

No, she said. *Not what I ask—you're a big boy now—what you ask of yourself. All I can do is point the way.* She studied him for a moment. *Be careful about making promises. You can deceive yourself.*

He'd gone a long way in that direction. Thinking that Ruthie hadn't seen through him. Thinking that he could just go ahead with the future and not have to look behind him—convinced that the truth would never come out. That what he did wouldn't matter. Thinking that his secret didn't carry any poison.

He was aware of something else. Ruthie wasn't going to yield up her confidences just because he'd called her and shown up. He'd have to woo her, invite her into himself. Otherwise he'd just have a few of her tricks. He was looking at the crow side of her. Awesome. She had magic on her side. She could look into past and future. He'd have to give himself to her before she'd give him the time of day. "Have you ever done that?" he asked her. "Deceived yourself?"

She cocked her head and looked at him. Her eye sparkled. *Does a crow have wings? We always think how the world should be—put our own pretty little faces on the scheme of things and think we know what's what.*

Now she was suggesting to him the riddle of her experience. And he was seeing her now as someone who indeed had had experience, holding the key to what he needed to know. He was looking for his own, in the little pack he carried and wasn't sure it had anything in it except a lot of noise and empty gestures. He was going to take a gamble. "You loved Pete," he said. "And he loved you."

She let out a melancholy squawk. *Awww. Deception and meanness of spirit,* she said. *We have it in us to be bigger than we are. But it takes all your life to get you there. And some of us never make it past the shadow.*

He noticed then his own shadow lying on the ground like an inkspot, and looked for hers. But he didn't see one. Had she cast that off too?

"Can you tell me?" He hoped his eagerness wouldn't scare her off.

There was a considering pause. *You know the end of the story,* she said. *Turn it on its head and it all funnels down into the beginning. Beginnings can be a bit sloppy. Well, you saw Lena when she was ailing and had lost nearly all her charms. But she was dynamite once. Me, I was never the looker. And she had the goods—sexy and lovely.*

She knew how to use the equipment better than anybody I ever knew. It came to her, naturally. She learned to walk with a swing of the hips from left to right, so that the guys panted after those curves all the way, they hoped, to a moist little paradise. And a face like a calendar photo. That was what she was. Beautiful—she had it in her to be that.

But we make beauty cheap, as though that's the way to power.

Honey for the flies. Beauty has a hard time becoming what it ought to be in the world. Thinks it has to be glitter. Thinks it has to be cheap. Thinks it has to put on the dog and pimp and whore for results. Plus you need a little help along the way, whether you choose the high road or the low road. And she was born into the wrong family to catapult her into the-sky's-the- limit. She had to go the back way, stealing fashion magazines from the library and the doctor's office so she could know all the latest fads and get-ups. Even when she was a little kid, she was draping stuff around her, shawls and going off as a princess. That's what she'd tell you, "I'm a princess."

When we lived on the reservation, we had our ways and traditions, though it was getting harder to keep hold of them. But when we moved into town, we could hardly keep ourselves going. In school we had all the white kids we had to compare ourselves to. Some were poor like us, but some had parents that were making it pretty good. Money for clothes and even a car. Maybe going to college. The t.v. promised you all kinds of good things.

Lena got it into her head she wanted to be a star and marry somebody rich. Maybe she thought that was a way of being somebody. She was beautiful, but she was still Indian and Mexican. Your mama was light-skinned. And you had a white father. You were a white boy. Only it didn't help all that much..

He had too many things to be mad about to pick out any one even to talk to anybody about.

Anyway, Lena figured she could get there, wherever there *is*, only if she went off to Hollywood. She took a hair styling course to make some money, figuring she could get a leg up doing hairdo's for the stars until she got "discovered." It was during the sixties, and some of us thought we could do anything. Only she didn't have a lot of talent for it. She couldn't act her way out of paper bag. She'd put on little shows at school, and some of the kids told her she was star material. All that went to her head.

And how was she going to manage in a place like L.A.? It made her depressed and made her fight for attention. And because she had a body she figured was a hot property and that she was bound to get some good out of it whether she made it to California or not.

So she set her sights on, a college dropout who was hanging around town looking for entertainment. His father owned string of hotels in Albuquerque. Phoenix, and L.A .who gave him anything he wanted—so he was somebody. Slick Eddie, I called him—because his hair was always slicked back, and he smelled of aftershave and had a neatly folded handkerchief in his pocket and money in his wallet. He had it all over the rest of us. Drove a fancy new convertible when anybody who even had wheels had his father's car he might occasionally borrow or an old jalopy

Eddie was a speed junkie, and it was a gamble to get into his car. He wrecked a couple of cars. But there was Daddy to pay for another one.

So where does Pete come into all this? Our families were close. We'd known each other from the beginning. Us kids played together, Pete and his older brother we called 'Horse,' Jake, Lena, and I. But Pete and I were special friends. We went down to the river to fish when we were big enough. We hiked along the trails and we went riding togeteher. We told things to each other we didn't tell anybody else. His mom and dad were ruined like us and moved into town when the mine spoiled their land. They started a bike shop, where you could buy a new bike or a used one and could have one fixed. They had a small house, nothing fancy.

In town, we'd meet sometimes for a coke. I'd complain about Lena and the boys getting into her pants. especially Eddie. At least that's what I figured. He was older than Lena and had been around. And I was sure he was going to *drop her right quick when he'd had what he wanted and was ready to move onto new territory. Pete had his troubles, too. Horse was getting into drugs, and Pete was worried about his mom because she was always tired. And cried sometimes.*

We'd all lost something moving into town. It was hard keeping hold of what the old life stood for—the ties to ceremony and our elders. We were dark-skinned people in a white world. We were made to feel ashame of what we were just by looking at those around us. We were brought up differently, and when we came together, we were wary, and they were wary, too. They were superior—you could tell from the way they walked. We huddled close to those who cared for us. It wasn't enough for Lena. She wanted the white world and what it offered.

I didn't know I loved Pete until we started dancing together. We'd go out to a place called the Blue Moon. Always crowded on the dance floor. Lena used to go there with her friends. She danced around and flirted with the guys. Stayed out late. I just danced with Pete. He'd asked me to go that first time. And we'd come together for a slow one, and I felt as though I'd just melted into him. I've never had that feeling with another man.

And he'd had it too, with Aline, those feelings he had no words for that were almost too much to bear. And because she accepted him for what he was, he was somebody.

"Lena wasn't interested in Pete?" Hawkins asked.

Not then. No, she'd never looked in his direction. He was too quiet, too serious. He wanted certain things. He was studying Spanish so he could go to Guatemala and help teach poor farmers how they could grow macadamia nuts and come to buy their own land. He wanted land too.. He had a friend down there who'd done well and wanted him to come down.

Yes. nothing out of the way in all this. Once she asked me what I saw in him. 'Something to make a future with. He's got a feeling for what he can do for himself and other people.' I loved that in him—and other things too. He made me happy. I loved being around him.

She made a sudden movement and flew up to a branch in one of the cottonwoods. *It was the night of the party that turned everything upside down. . We'd never really been to a party like this one. Feasts and ceremonies for the pueblo— This was different. it was Lena who insisted that we go. 'A real party,' she said.*

It was at Slick Eddie's house, and the only thing we were celebrating was that the house was all his, and he could do as he pleased. His folks were out in L.A. at his father's hotel. 'I got everything you could ask for,' he said and pulled open the doors of a cabinet. A whole cabinet full of booze. Fancy bottles of stuff I'd never seen before. Pretty. too. with all their labels—gleaming in various colors, red, amber, yellow. One had a pale lovely green liquor inside, and I told Pete that if we drank it we'd turn into butterflies. We were both having a beer. "What d'you think a beer will change you into?" he said.

I'd seen what booze could turn you into. There was a friend of Dad's, I guess you could call him a friend—somebody he knew from the mine. He'd come by wanting Dad to go out drinking with him. Drunk a lot of the teime. He'd stagger over, though I will say he could hold his booze. My dad would drive him home and he and his wife would pour coffee into him. Some of the boys at school would clump together and drink till they were they were puking drunk. I saw some of that. I'll bet you did your share. Paved your way into trouble, I'll bet. But then you were ready for it.

A tremor went through him. He was always having to prime himself. Scoop himself up out of the familar pit. To greater daring. He, too, must have been ashamed of what he was.

Everybody was into the booze. We were hanging onto that one beer. I didn't like the taste of whiskey, and Pete wasn't a drinker. I guess he was looking too sober for Eddie and the rest of the guys, a spoil-sport. So they started in on him. He wasn't any kind of man if he couldn't take in a little whiskey. He'd have to take one shot at least. He said no, this wasn't his kind of party, and he was going home. They razzed him and taunted him and wouldn't let him go till he'd had one good shot. They poured one, probably more than that into a beer and made him chug it down. 'Chug-a-lug,' they were yelling. They'd have poured it down his throat. They tried to goad him to take another, but he pushed it away. Tried to get up so he could leave.

"You got to get initiated," they were yelling and holding onto him and pushing him off in the direction of the bedroom. I hadn't seen Lena for a while. And what-do-you know, she's in there, too drunk to know what she's doing, just whooping and hollering, and the guys are taking turns having a go at her. I tried to go in and get her out of there, but the guys wouldn't let me

interfere. Some of the other girls had pulled out and gone home on their own. A couple of the others were having the time of their lives. But three of us stormed in the bedroom and put a stop to it. Pete came staggering out, looking dazed, as if he didn't know where he was. Some of the guys were throwing up in the bathroom. One of them boasted he'd had ten beers. We all got home in some fashion—call it a miracle. I drove Pete's car. I figured we were lucky to get back in one piece.

Hawkins wasn't surprised by what she'd told him about Lena. He'd thought of her simply as part of a couple, of which the other half was Pete. But Ruthie had given him something to connect to his own experience. Nor was he surprised when she told him the rest of the story—how a couple of months later she told Ruthie she was pregnant. At first, she said it was Eddie, but, though Ruthie was sure it could have been him or any of the others, she told their mother it was Pete. Ruthie wouldn't believe it. But then Lena had to know Eddie wouldn't marry her, and the others she hardly knew. *I wanted to strangle her*, Ruthie said. *She was the winner in the game.*

It was a terrible blow for his parents. *Broke Angela's heart. She thought great things were in her son. That's how mothers are. They have their dreams, too. She was hoping for a scholarship for him tp go to the university. If he married Lena and had a kid right off the bat, he was going to have to get a job and postpone what he wanted or give it up entirely. And I was sure it wasn't his child. The booze went right to his head, he told me, and he couldn't remember anything after that.*

I believed him, but Lena wouldn't change her story. She had a whole description worked out. He was the only one who went all the way. Our folks and Pete's talked the whole thing over and finally it was arranged the two would marry.

I never wanted anything to do with Lena. And maybe I blamed Pete for falling under her spell. Because I think he did that. Maybe he touched something of that beauty she had and wanted to hold onto it. Like I said, beauty has a hard time in the world—maybe always has. And I suspect Lena knew how to please a man.

But I wasn't about to let go of Pete, you see, not entirely. There was a bond between us, and I needed something to carry with me. I planned the way things were going to work. I wanted that much—a marriage. A secret marriage that nobody'd know about. There's more than one person in the world you can love, but I knew Pete was the only one for me. Before he and Lena cast their lot, I arranged what we would do, and he was willing. We went off together and had one night of bliss. And your mother was born out of that night. I was all alone when she came along—my Annie. I'd gone off to Denver to work in a bar up there, Lena and Pete were living with our folks. I didn't leave any address. *She was what I knew of joy. Everything changes.*

"Don't go," Hawkins pleaded as he saw her rise into the air. She sailed. around once

You've got all I can give you. All you're going to get. The fledgling is out of the nest. You gonna fly or fall to the ground and get eaten by the cat? Finally, it's all one to the Great One weaving the net. But I believe in you— you've got a few coals still glowing. If you want to get out of the mess you're in, you in, you've got to go to the Snake People. Not that it'll be easy—never is. After all, you were the one to leave the door open for them. That rattler you've got on your arm . . . A clear invitation.

And she rose and disappeared.

X

Snake people. He cringed at the thought. Was something coming to him—a punishment for the tattoo he'd flaunted, paid for with part of Ruthie's household money he'd swiped from her purse? So that now they were after him? A good thing he hadn't gotten tattoos on both arms. He'd heard how rattlesnakes came in pairs, and if you messed with one, the other just lay in wait for you, ready to strike. He was in snake territory all right, he could hear a hissing around him as chills traveled down his spine. *You have come here to the snake people because there is no other place for you to go. We counsel you to marry the Snake Maiden.*

He stood uncertainly, his legs refusing the impulse to flee. When he looked up from his turmoil, he saw that he was standing near a cleft in the rock, a cave half-hidden that presented one more darkness to enter or the curse of waiting for something deadly to emerge. Doomed. It was as though he'd been thrown out of time, or sucked into some deep pocket of it he'd never known. Yet he felt the beating of his blood, even though everything around him seemed to be standing still. Even his body had turned into a mystery. He felt boneless and without weight or even identity.

Enter the stillness. The words hung in the air, as though he might step into some space beyond movement, in which the past would melt and all desire evaporate. If only he could get rid of the confusion in his head and the hard knot that lay at his core. He could almost catch a glimpse of another world that kept teasing him, as it receded like a mirage. This was Chaco Canyon, and he could no longer say what it held, what could happen there.

"Help me," he whispered. "What am I supposed to do now?"

Just be patient, the voice told him, as if it were speaking to a child, taking hold of him once more. *The Snake People are preparing a ceremony for you.*

"But the snake maiden . . ."

All in good time. Sit down and calm yourself. After all, you've lived a long time with that snake. Why did you put it on your body if you were going to ignore it? Think of the insult.

Insult!—when all he wanted was to show people he was mean and tough? A kid thing. He wished he'd never seen the damned tattoo.

When they're ready, they'll come for you.

Oh, great. He'd get to twiddle his thumbs while they made him sweat. Keep him standing there till he was swimming in snakes. It was a good time to check out. He had half a mind just to get into the truck and take off. The stone? He could toss it into the sagebrush and pretend the whole thing had never happened, that he'd dreamed it and everything else. None of it seemed real anyway.

You've got this far . . . he was reminded. But he was already aware he'd regret it if he just took off and kept on running. Where had it got him except to the edge of a cliff, ready to step off?

Reluctantly, he sat down on a flat rock, looked around blankly—nothing there to do with himself for how long?—then reached for a stick lying on the ground not far from him and began making lines in the sandy soil.

A ceremony? He'd already seen one ceremony—the drums and the dancers, the masked figures that were gods, yet men. He hadn't really thought what it all added up to. People believed such things were real.

He took a moment to look into the day. The leaves of the cottonwoods were beginning to pale and kept sailing down from the branches. The warmth at the edge of the afternoon was a deception. He wondered how long it would take before the cold took over the day altogether, when no campers would come, except perhaps someone as desperate as himself. The animals would all retreat into their burrows, the white butterfly sink into the frost. Maybe it had already.

He stood up and walked around idly, let his eye wander over the surroundings. Just beyond him, a great white cloud towered up above the butte, against the turquoise sky. He was surrounded by all that rose beyond him, the cottonwoods, great buttes, the bank of cloud.

He sat down again to wait, all thought congealed and picked the stick again to make his own petroglyphs on the ground. Something made a little rustle in the dry grass nearby, and when he looked closely, he saw a horny toad. He hadn't seen one for a long time, the brown figured body with the white underbelly, the head with its triangular horns. As a kid he used to pick them up and carry them around. They had come from another world, almost beyond time, an odd creature left over from the dinosaurs. How had they managed to survive when so many creatures had gone under along the way? And did this one carry a jewel in its head? Was that what the Anasazi saw? It sat unmoving, but kept a steady bead on him, very likely hoping to escape notice. With his stick he nudged it over on its back, and it lay there, making no protest. He began to tickle its belly with the end of the stick. It simply lay there—what would he have to do to get a rise out of it?

Don't do that, the voice came with warning. *Otherwise a storm will come and delay the ceremony.*

Was somebody shitting him? For good measure, he gave the horned toad one more poke as it lay helpless on its back. Then, annoyed, he flipped the creature over and watched it scurry off in the grass.

A chill came into the air. Somehow the blue of the sky with its strong sun to began to fade into gray, the great white cloud to darken as he watched. Other clouds began to gather seemingly out of nowhere, until they made a dark mat across the sky. Moments later he heard the rattle of thunder not that far away. A flash of lightning split the sky.

Just as he realized he'd better take shelter, the rain came pelting down, wetting him as he raced toward the cleft he'd noticed earlier. He stepped back into its shelter, where he stood watching the rain turn into a screen of water he could hardly see through. He wanted to laugh—that he and the horny toad could have anything to do with the rain, that there could be any possible connection. Just inside, where he could barely see the outlines of things, he found a shelf of rock where he could sit. Clearly, he was in for a wait.

He closed his eyes and sank back into the sound of the downpour.

Through the rain came a hissing of voices. *You've turned things upside down and inside out. Everything backward. What are you trying to do, control the weather? You've tried to control everything else, all the wrong way. Are you trying to be a god?*

He had no idea whether they were talking directly to him or beyond him. What could he have done? Something he'd blundered into all unknowing? He was at a loss. The voices trailed off and receded in the distance, but not before one last question assailed him, *You think you understand how everything works in the universe?* The rain continued its pounding in front of him, thunder sounded as if the earth were breaking apart. Every once in a while the mouth of the cave exploded with light.

He waited a long time, listening to the monotonous downpour, wondering if it would ever stop. Gradually, it began to taper off, and then to subside, and he was left to his own absurdities. He saw himself sitting inside the wall of the cave carving his own petroglyphs into the rock. There was a woman giving birth, the figure of a man holding a knife, a journey suggested by several figures, a family, a wandering, a confusion of roads and signs—small explosions, large ones, deaths. Crows.

He was part of the long line of those who had moved past carrying their lives with them, making their journeys. Every time he picked up a piece of his life, it came with a whole past clinging to it that might well go back to the dinosaurs. With him knowing nothing of it, and yet in some peculiar way, it was putting its stamp on him, as well as others.

The air was close, his breathing slowed, and he could hardly keep his eyes open. Another set of images entered his vision. And he heard what seemed to be a chorus of voices. *There have been others like you. Long ago one of them came to us. For him, nothing was sacred, and he did as he pleased. He followed no law. He didn't believe the gods existed, only men who pretended they were the gods . He was on his way to the underworld to see whether his tribesmen had been deceiving him. The elders told him to marry the snake maiden, and then it happened—a union between man and snake.*

He couldn't be sure what he was seeing, man and snake were dissolving together, then separating. Yet something seemed to hold them in union.

Most of you don't come near us. There are some who are bitten and die—a few who can cast off what is dead. . . .

He jerked up, for some movement had given him a start, perhaps a creature that made its home there. He stood up to stretch his legs, relieve his butt from the hard rock. The cave, he saw, tunneled back to unknown depths, no light anywhere. He could no longer see outside. The space seemed to close around him, the air thick with the smell of mold and decay. He was desperate for air—he'd take his chances outside. He could get only so wet. He'd just follow the line of the cliff and find his way back to his spot underneath by the little dwelling, but the rain had blown in and made a slippery mess under his feet as he tried for the exit. His feet slipped out from under him, and he slid into a wide depression wet and slippery at the bottom. It was difficult for him to gain a purchase as he tried to climb out.

How did you get into this mess? a familiar voice asked him. *When are you going to get it right? You can't live down here. Use your head.*

Live? At the moment, light and air would be sufficient. He'd already scraped his hands and knees. He pushed himself forward, dug in the toes of his boots, felt around for something to cling to, got a toehold, and struggled to lift himself up. He pushed with his feet and got over the edge to where he could crawl forward, just crawl in the direction of the opening, using his fingers like claws, chilled with the wet, covered with mud—till he managed to reach the opening. He lay there for a time, panting, trying to take back his breath from what he smelled on the floor of the cave, bat shit maybe—past loss and violence and folly. For their imprints lay on the walls of the cave,

They sprang into view, like a reel unwinding, as he passed them, giving off their own eerie light. Images he could go on replaying forever. He had to breathe his way past them, breathe powerfully. Now he wanted to move beyond what had shaped him—and live, if he could find out what living was.

Don't stop here, the voice urged him. *You've got to get out.*

He didn't know how long it took him to reach the opening, but when he did, it had stopped raining, and the sky had cleared. He stood up, took in a deep breath, hardly able to believe he'd made it.

Nothing's guaranteed.

A rattlesnake lay coiled in front of him. It had not given warning but raised up and fixed him with its eye. *You've been a long time getting here.*

He knew he was in danger but the only place he could run was back into the cave. In the past, he'd have grabbed a rock or a shovel to beat it off. You couldn't kill too many snakes. It blocked his way, and no weapon was handy. The hair stiffened at the back of his neck. Then carefully he stepped back, trying to convince the snake he would do no harm. It was a large diamondback, with a beautiful geometry of intersecting shapes along its coils. "Look, I don't want any trouble."

So, the rattler said, *you have my image on your arm. You've made us your totem?*

Hawkins had all but forgotten the tattoo. A totem? He hardly knew what it signified, let alone that he'd be taken into account. An image of power. An announcement: he's dangerous, he can strike, he can kill you.

You've trampled on my territory, the snake hissed. *Humans are good at that. Without respect.* There was movement in the coils.

He was being offered another chance for death. All he had to do was take a single step and be done with it. A certain mockery confronted him.

"I just need . . ."

What do you need? The snake was bearing down on him, though it hadn't moved. *You've stolen something for yourself you've never earned.*

And the job isn't even done well. Dead. Without feeling, without beauty. Are you dense enough to think my people haven't been wronged?

Smitty had done his best—the design had been in a catalogue. It hurt like bloody fury. He couldn't try to make any claims.

But you've got poison in you. The real stuff.

Poison. Like a snake's? Running in his veins?

Yes, I see you'd like to get rid of it. That takes some doing. First the burning—what do you know of fire? Then the distilling. Our poison can heal—did you know that?

Lots of people had been bit and died, including those who meant no harm.

You've been down in a hole. That's where we come from. Our domain, where the secrets of the earth lie. True knowledge. We hear the news from underground. The whole history of the earth. So you've learned to respect what will kill you. You think that's enough?

He had no answer. He shifted onto one foot and watched her make a move, threatening. *Know me now as the snake maiden.* She shot forward, and he fell back and sank to the ground. Whether or not she had struck him, a fire burned through his veins, and it seemed his heart and breath would die in the flames. Everything caught fire and burned away. Like scraps of paper, hollow shapes. As it all burned and disintegrated, he recognized that none of it had really belonged to him, but that he had clung to it because he didn't know any better. He stood in the burning, closed his eyes, and let it happen. The pain of it seemed almost a form of happiness. He was ready to step out of his skin.

XI.

When he came back to himself, it wasn't clear where he'd been or for how long. What seemed to happen over a span of days was perhaps no more than a blur across his inner eye, so that he could not separate dream from waking. Time, which had led him through the durations of sun, moon and stars, perhaps held other dimensions he seemed to be both inside and outside of.

Now as he regained his feet, the sun was shining brilliantly, with little trace of the rain that had inundated things before. Except for a few puddles, which shone like mirrors, the ground appeared dry, though there was mud on his boots and he could hear the rush of water through the wash. The Snake Maiden was nowhere in sight, though he sensed her presence and then heard her voice. *Now you must come for the ceremony.*

A group of men and boys had paused a little distance from him, and their leader beckoned him to approach. He moved to where they waited and fell in behind them. He followed them past the trailhead that was to take him to Pueblo Alto, as they spoke to one another, gesturing occasionally. They continued on at a faster pace across a gently rising stretch of land studded with sage and clumps of cactus, then through a canyon where he was arrested by a large petroglyph on a tall flat rock. A figure stood with bow in hand, a circle emerging; two diverging paths opened beyond, one filled with figures, smaller circles near the other. He paused to take in the images. First things first, the voice of the Snake Maiden reminded him. In time you'll have room for prophecy.

He turned back to the path, from which he could see the outlines of a pueblo. He could hear sounds of activity and other voices, an occasional shout—a living pueblo, its walls bearing some resemblance to what he had seen in Pueblo Bonito. As he approached the cliff he was to climb, the noises of community life became sharper, more abundant. There was increasing activity around him as shadowy figures began to take form, to exist in a different light.

When he arrived at the pueblo with his companions, he found himself among a group of people making prayer sticks and sand paintings. *The Snake and the Antelope clans,* the Snake Maiden told him. *You need both,* she said. *What comes from down below—cold, from the ground. And warm—the warm blood of he animal.* Snake energies to begin with, then going all the way up.

He watched while one of the men directed sand through his fingers to create the borders of red, white, green and yellow on the four sides of the painting. Within were semi-circles that reminded Hawkins of clouds, snake-like zigzags that looked like lightning, and slashes like falling rain. *Do you see,* she said, *we are here for the rain. Prayers to make the earth green again.*

He saw one of the men pick up a green corn stalk and set it in the middle, and others set green corn stalks and bowls of water about an altar.

With his companions, Hawkins moved out into the bush in the direction of another group, men and boys with sticks, looking closely about them and bending down into the grass. When he was close enough, he saw one of the boys lift a snake, holding it behind its head. Another, who looked to be a priest, came up, stroked the back of the snakes with a wand of feathers to keep it from coiling. The priest moved about calming the snakes.

Hawkins watched the boys working with the men, plunging their sticks into snake holes and capturing the rattlers, bull snakes, and gopher snakes that emerged, along with those they surprised among the rocks. They simply seized hold of them and dropped them in their snake sacks. Dozens of snakes. One had been too many for him, Hawkins thought, and and that one hadn't let go of him yet. He could sense a certain satisfaction on her part as he stood in the midst of all the activity, hoping none of the snakes would move in his direction. He was fascinated and yet horrified, as he watched the men search out the snakes, digging them out of their holes, stroking their backs with feathers until they hung limp, and safely depositing them. Why were they going after them? he wondered. Why so many? How would it be to take part himself?

What would they ask him to do?

It was a while before he found out. Though a great wave of relief came over him when the snake-hunting was over, and the snakes were deposited at a shrine built to hold them, a hole dug for them and covered with a blanket, after they'd been fed with corn and pollen. That task was finished, but the Snake People were not done with him.

First there was the waiting. For hours, it seemed, he sat alone, apart, while the men did a ceremony in the Antelope kiva, for the lower had to come to the higher, the Snake Maiden told him, and he could not enter there.

When they summoned him again, the men were sitting in a circle in the kiva, knee to knee. They created a space for him to sit, as their chanting rose around him. Staggered, he was seeing what he had been summoned for: the release of the snakes on the sand in the center, wriggling and crawling as the men continued their chant.

How could it be? Just sitting there singing away like they were in Sunday School. He held his breath. But he couldn't hold it forever. He knew, if he wanted to live, he had to sit calmly like the others, not give way to fear or loathing or any violence in him. He could feel his heart pounding, as he tried to hold onto the calm the other men displayed, as the snakes, first taking their bath in the sand, started crawling toward them. They began crawling over the men's bodies, as the men sat in their stillness. Two of them crawled up into one man's lap and curled up to sleep there, the host was so entirely relaxed and accepting. Others crawled over the men's knees, along their backs and down their chests.

One was crawling toward Hawkins, the diamondback that had been in the cave. *Now you can know me as I know you. How will you receive me?*

She crawled up his leg, around his knee and up his thigh, exploring him. He could feel his genitals recoil as though to hide inside him. His muscles were tense; he held his breath. Then as she circled his waist, crawled up his back and coiled around his shoulders like a shawl, he exhaled slowly and somehow let go. She was there, but he didn't mind her being there. He sat with her, breathing with her and forgot himself—they were one creature. The chanting took him over. Then he felt her move down the center of his chest, onto his thigh and down into the sand. She left him with a word, *Only surrender.*

As she disappeared among the other snakes, he felt a kindling of energies, a surge of power she had brought from the earth to his own lower depths. He could feel the energy of it in his body— and then a feeling of joy.

He is carried along in the momentum of that energy into first one, then another part of the ceremony—the ritual wedding of the Snake Maiden and Antelope Youth. He sees the young girl enter in her black dress and red and white cape, her face painted with black and white. She is more than a young woman; she is the Snake goddess he saw at the altar of the kiva. She comes from the moon and the darkness. In her lies a power to create. She carries a jar containing prayer sticks, and corn, and melon, squash, and beans. vines. Everything holds a meaning, a mystery that everyone there is part of.

There is the youth, his body painted ash gray, a white line across his chin. He holds a snake. Each holds what belongs to the other. He watches as the maiden's dark hair is washed in yucca milk by the chiefs of the Snake clan, braided with the hair of the youth, also wet from milk. Here is their union, the union of Snake and Antelope. They are conducted to a seating ledge, where the girl sits upon a plaque of seeds—for the birds, the animals and human beings. The chanting begins that will last until the stars in Orion's belt hang over the Western horizon

Hawkins is exhausted, yet energized with a power that is new to him. His head is crowded with all that now passe before him. First the races of the Antelope men, who have come from miles around, making a thunder with their running to awaken the rain clouds. Then the dancers. First the priest approaching the shrine with its its intertwined snakes, seizing one behind the head with his teeth, then handing each of the men a snake. Two rows of twelve dancers, each man holding a snake, shaking their rattles as they circle the plaza to the thunder of drums, while the men,women and children of the pueblo eagerly entering the experience. Snake and Antelope now joined, the snakes are released to re-enter the bush.

Again there are faces, the faces of women wavering in front of him: his mother with her dark hair and tender mouth; hard-bitten Ruthie; Lena, her face contorted in pain; Marietta, the wanderer with her children; Aline in her grace and fury. They come, one superimposed on the other. Then they are all gathered into the image of the Snake Maiden, the young girl with her flowing hair. But something more, something of great magnitude that holds rock and stone, plant and animal, and a shadowy emerging figure that includes all the faces of women and men. Curiously, the words "father" and "mother" no longer belong to him as a source of pain—they all have slipped away, and he sees within himself something that holds everything together, as abiding as stone.

The rattlesnake is there again. *It's time,* she says, changing before his eyes, growing feathers and wings, taking flight. *It's time.* Apparently for him. Without knowing what is happening, he is casting off his dead skin and giving birth to himself.

XII.

He opened his eyes to a sense of difference, not yet clear about where he had been. Whatever his experience, it would take a while to know its dimensions. He felt amazement. He was looking about with that amazement—amazed to find himself there in one piece, to see that the sun was tilting toward the west, lighting up the horizon before sunset, that the leaves of the cottonwoods were aglow and the plants that left their dry twigs around him, were subsiding into their seeds and roots, another season spent. He felt a pleasant sense of emptiness that seemed somehow filled with richness, as though he'd been delivered of a burden he had carried for a long time and now had space for something else. He was left with a wordless stillness and a certain clarity. Words were like another country, another territory of mind, and he was sitting uncertainly at the borders.

He was aware that there was the wind to listen to, and the sounds of birds, leaving their imprint on the late afternoon. He wasn't certain whether he was in the world or out of it. But then the crows entered his consciousness once more, flying over the day as usual. He sensed warning in their cries, and the voice was again speaking in his ear. *It's not easy to balance the two worlds. Step with caution.*

"Here, let me help you, amigo." He hadn't heard anyone approach, but here was someone bending over him. He was looking up into the face of a stranger—the mouth smiling; above it, a large red nose with hairs in the nostrils, overseen by eyes sharp as picks, a face clean-shaven, smoothed with aftershave. The owner, a man in a dark brown cowboy hat, a handsome suede jacket over a western shirt, pants that bowled around his paunch, and elaborately tooled boots to house his feet.

"What happened to you, amigo—you stumble over a rock?'

"Here, give me your hand," he said, holding out a thick palm.

"Wait a minute," Hawkins said. "I'm okay . . . I was . . . just out of time."

It was all he could think to say.

"I'll say you were. They want you off those mesas before sundown. Don't want anybody getting hurt wandering around in the dark. They close up the whole place. You feeling woozy from the sun? Climbed too high too fast?"

"No," he said. It was too simple a matter to take on explanation. He was simply sitting there on the ground near his truck in the parking space for Pueblo Bonito. He had been somewhere else.

"Looks like you could use a drink. I'm in that shape myself. I've got stuff back in the r.v.," the stranger said. "Name's Everett D. Thornton. A turn-around from Thornton D. Everett. Comes down harder that way. D stayed where it was. You can call me E.D."

The voice dinned in his ears as the other insisted on being helpful. " I can offer you a pick-me-up," he said with a laugh. "Scotch or bourbon. Top of the line. In fact, I've got a little something right here if you want a nip." He passed over Hawkins' silence. "Here," he said, still with his palm extended. Hawkins allowed himself to be hoisted up. Once up, he'd have a chance to escape.

"After what I've been through today I sorely need a drink—two, in fact. You up for it?"

"No, better not," Hawkins mumbled.

"Whats the matter—you sick or something?" he said, as though that could be the only reason for refusing a drink.

"No," Hawkins said. "Just waking up, I guess you could say." He was feeling an increasing need to be alone. A sudden cough came over him as though he were about to be choked by a desert wind.

"Want a cigarette?" the stranger offered him, pulling out a pack.

"No thanks." The very thought of tobacco revolted him.

The stranger felt around in his pocket. "Damn. Must have lost my lighter. You wouldn't happen to have a match?"

Matches. He did have some and pulled a matchbook out of his pocket.

"Okay, I'll match you for them. Match you for the matches. Thornton said with a laugh.

"Take them," Hawkins said.

"No, no. You call it. Heads, I get the matches—tails, you lose."

What was he trying to pull? "Wait a minute—I've got to light my fire."

"Okay, okay—my little joke. I've got some back in the r.v."

He took the matches from Hawkins and lit his cigarette. "You from around here?" he asked, as Hawkins adjusted himself to a standing position. "Been through Pueblo Bonito?" A whole series of questions rolled out of him. Did he have a campsite and what trails had he'd been on? Had he seen any of the Navajos that worked there?

Hawkins was dumbfounded, inundated as much by the stream of talk as by the words themselves.

"Yeah," he said, "I'm out here for a little r and r, in my r.v." That tickled him too, and he let go again with his high, moist laugh. "Hellova day," he said, "trying to sell a good deal. Think about that. Those Indians sitting on all kinds of wealth and they won't do what's good for them. Jobs galore just waitng for them."

He paused to let Hawkins to take that in. "Used to be our government was boss, only now they got these tribal councils and lawyers, just like everybody else, and you can't budge 'em."

He wasn't about to stop until he'd delivered himself of his grievance, but Hawkins couldn't listen—not to him or anyone else.

"Yeah, well, sorry about that—I got to go take a leak and set up my fire," he said, turning away, moving toward his truck.

He drove slowly around the loop back to the campground. Up ahead, he saw what at first he thought were two dogs bounding across the road. Then he recognized them—coyotes. He'd never seen a pair of them together. He speeded up a little to see them more closely, but they were at the other road when he reached them. He could see only one of them, which had paused and was staring up at him.

He'd heard stories about Coyote and his mischief. He hoped none was brewing for him. He needed a quiet night.

Ahead of him, Fajada Butte was aglow, struck by the lowering sun. He hoped the moon would rise beyond it.

When he reached his campsite, he remembered that he hadn't collected his matches. Or maybe that was E.D.'s way of winning .The only vehicle there was an r.v., parked in the site next to his, and he realized he'd just encountered his neighbor.

The air was already chill, as he began to lay out the kindling for his fire, hoping his neighbor would show up with his matches. He got his sleeping bag out of the truck and laid it out under the cliff near the little dwelling. He had the feeling he'd probably be spending a good part of the night watching the stars.

His neighbor pulled in, got out of his car and came toward him.

"You took off in such a hurry...," he said handing him his matches. "You sure you won't have that drink?"

"Stomach problems," Hawkins said, and knelt down to light the fire. His hands were trembling.

"Well, too bad," Thornton said. "I don't suppose I could interest you in a bowl of chili. I got more than I can use."

One match went out, then another. "Here, let me do that," Thornton said, taking the matches from him. "You got a fever?"

"No, just a chill." The fire caught, and Hawkins knelt close to it, trying to warm up.

"A chill but no chili," Thornton said, slapping his thigh. "That's a good one, isn't it? Don't mind me—it's in the blood. Hold on," he said, "I've got a blanket in there. Real Navajo. They charge an arm and a leg for them these days." The man was getting on his nerves, even though he meant well.

A moment later, he reappeared, blanket in hand, gray, white and black, covered with a diamond design that reminded Hawkins of the rattler. Gratefully, he wrapped it around him.

"You look like an Indian yourself," Everett said, "but with a pale face. A pale-face Indian." He gave his belly-shaking laugh.

Hawkins was still shivering.

"Come on, take a little snort of this—it'll warm you up." Thornton took a flask from his coat pocket. "It'll be a cold night."

Before he knew what he was doing, the liquor was in his mouth and burning in his chest. Its heat entered the chill, and the two seemed to mingle within him.

Meanwhile the stranger had sat down on the bench of the picnic table. "I don't know what sort of shape you're in," he said, "but I'll be glad to help out if I can. This is a lonesome place, you know. Not a soul around here tonight. People got to help each other."

"I appreciate it," Hawkins said, "but I'll be fine with this blanket and the fire. I don't like to bother people."

"Hell, it's no bother. Just being neighborly. I'm pretty beat out myself. Nice to have somebody to talk to. You know, those Indians'll drive 90 miles an hour down the road in their pickups while they're all boozed up, yet they won't take the risk of a good solid working uranium mine that'll give them a living. Isn't that crazy?"

"They have their own way of living," Hawkins said, wanting to defend them.

"Bullshit," Thornton said. "Some of them are poor as dirt—can't even feed their families. And they'd have more than jobs—they'd get royalties. Some of that land isn't worth shit—can't farm it, can't even raise sheep."

"Wait a minute," Hawkins said, his hackles rising. "A bunch of them got sick—uranium in their water and on the land. My grandmother died of cancer—she wasn't all that old. She looked like a skeleton towards the end. And her folks died of it. They had land, good land, and after it was leased foe mining, it was ruined. The water was poisoned, and everybody got sick."

"Hold on. That was a long time ago. Now they got all this new technology. Don't even have to blast or dig pits—Just suck the stuff out with water and pump clear water back in." He'd been trying to explain all that so the ones interested could convince the tribal council, and they were all excited about it.

He wasn't in the mood to argue. It still sounded like a poor idea.

"What happened to that land?" Thornton wanted to know.

Hawkins shrugged. "It's no good." After Ruthie died, Clyde had handed him the lease. "Make something out of that if you can.

Maybe a little blood money—if you don't end up in the slammer first."

He hadn't punched Clyde, or torn up the lease, maybe because it had been a part of Ruthie's life. It had the names of her father and mother on it. As close as he'd ever get to his ancestors.

"Listen," Thornton said, "I'd be interested in seeing what you've got. Might be a good prospect for us both."

"It's gone," he said. He'd left everything back in his room, then left without paying the rent. Who knew what the landlady had done with his things? Hawkins moved out of the smoke, so that his back was to Thornton. He was hoping Thornton would leave, but the man hadn't done with him yet.

"I'm buying up land I can get cheap. A base for operations. Because I got a few of the smart ones fighting the tribal counci. They want the jobs—they have good sense. None of those council guys would talk to me—just turned their backs on me and said they'd fight to the death. Told me to get off their land and keep on going. Damn it all, that's how they treat a friend."

"You work for a mining company?"

"You're damned right I do. Not only work for it, I represent it. Me and my partners started it. Started it from nothing but a little know-how. There's money, big money to be made on those lands. They got uranium like Saudi Arabia's got oil. And there's a world out there waiting to build nuclear plants right and left.

So he'd come to do the Indians another favor. The whole scheme smelled bad to him.

"I think I'm okay now," Hawkins said, removing the blanket and handing it to him.

Thornton stood up, too. "Well, I'll go get me some supper," he said. "You got food?"

"I can't eat right now," Hawkins said. He felt dizzy, wanted only to be alone.

"Well, if you need anything, give me a yell." Thornton said, turning off to his r.v.

As he sat back down by the fire, Hawkins thought of Ruthie

during one of her tirades years ago after she'd read an article in the paper. "Those companies promise you the world—jobs and royalties. And what did we get?—sickness and death—for our land, our sheep, our kids. The tribe fought for years to get them to come and clean up the mess they made. Fat lot of good it did."

He was glad for the silence that now surrounded him. Lights were on in Thornton's r.v., and he could smell chili cooking. A nearly full moon was rising.

XIII.

He remembered crawling into his sleeping bag, but it did not offer a place of refuge. His surroundings seemed to be on fire, as though a poison had spread throughout. The voice that had been with him from the first seemed to be speaking out of the flames: *The poison was in you, but you've been purged by the fire that burns it away. Only now the whole world is on fire.* He could see flames filling the sky, burning through the air, spreading on the earth, even the sea, wtth birds and fish washed to the shore. He saw the yellow dust blowing across the desert, breathed in by a the living creatures there, running into the water and then the soil. He saw sheep eating the plants that contained it. Sheep and people born with sightless eyes and twisted limbs Everything caught up in the burning.

Another voice assailed him. *Take a gamble. You want a better world, a better life? Come on, friends. We got to move forward, not look behind. Progress—never forget it. Things change. You want to save a few tribes and animals from going extinct, a bunch of folks holding onto dead land?* Thornton's face loomed over him, his voice above the fire. *It isn't nature's way. Hell, she's been destroying critters from the git-go. Have we got any dinosaurs tromping around? Only In the museums, where they belong. And a few still hobbling along, bones creaking in their pitiful skeletons. They'd pull us back to the Stone Age, if we let 'em. Set loose the sabre-tooth tigers and wooly mammoths so they could eat us or stomp us to death—is that better?"*

Thornton was doing a little dance in front of him, a swaying dance, light on his feet for a man of his girth, working his head from side to side, waving his arms slightly with his body's motion. *What have we done? I ask you. What have we done? Taken fertilizer to the fields, pesticides to the pests and fed the world. That's what we've done.*

The voice rose in a chant. *Tell, me—tell me, what have we done?"* Swaying with his chant. *Found cures for all that ails you— Look about, just look about you—look at all the drugs on the pharmacy shelves. For the heart and lungs, the liver and lights. What have we done? Seen into the mysteries of mind and body. Taken parts out, split them up, made them whole and put them back— even put others in their place. We've taken the gamble, used our wits—given folks back a whole new life. Helped children walk and blind men see.*

We've conquered oceans and swept the skies. Gone to the moon. Walked on Mars. What'll you do now? Turn back the clock? Make fire with flint and steel or two sticks rubbed together? Hell, there are other things I'd rather rub together, make a sweet little fire.

He winked, gave one more twist and then sat himself down, breathless, fixing Hawkins with his eye, grinning, weaving his spell. *What's your name, fella? You got one? Did you come to this earth to live on it or are you just sitting on the pot? Ready to gamble? Scared you'll lose?*

His eyes were electric. There was power in them as he held Hawkins in his glare. Gamble, what did he have to gamble? Scared of losing what? What did he have to be afraid of?

Now after a night that left him uneasy, Hawkins was at the picnic table with bread on a plate, a cup of coffee at his elbow.

"You look dry in the mouth," Thornton said, "Here, drink a little of this—perk you up a bit. A little breakfast special to wet things down and warm the blood, perk up the liver." He took the flask from his jacket pocked and poured some into Hawkins' cup. "Purest stuff money can buy."

What sort of stuff? Hawkins wondered, as he picked up the cup. He took a sip and set the cup down.

"You got something against a little play for fun? Just to enjoy the company?" Thornton laughed. "It goes back to the cave man. As soon as he could make a cry, he picked up his bone dice and tried for his fortune. The Lady with the Wheel—sometimes up and sometimes down. And been doing it ever since. Right here, in these rooms, they've discovered bone dice and gaming sticks. Had all sorts of contests. Think of that. Those guys knew how to play, and I'll bet they made a good time of it."

Hawkins had tried his luck at poker now and then, played some pool with the guys he ran with. Lost some money at it. Maybe the other things he'd done were a gamble, it occurred to him. Stealing change, lifting hubcaps, breaking into the convenience store. Gambling against getting caught, putting up some part of himself on the line, a piece of his life—something that would change what came next. The air began to melt in front of him. He was hardly there for Thornton, who would go on talking in any case. Only a presence was necessary—maybe he preferred his silence to talk into.

"All those Indians gambled—part of their religion. Only now they got casinos—more my style. They're making money hand over fist. And I got my eye in that direction." He leaned toward Hawkins confidentially. "Bought me a piece of land, fifty miles from here. Gonna build a resort—250-room hotel, golf course, swimming pool, and a casino. Just as soon as my next ship comes in. Texans'll flock there like birds of prey. Like those crows overhead. It's my big dream."

Hawkins looked at him in wonder. Nothing of that scale had ever crossed his mind. He'd enjoyed a few fantasies playing video games or watching the flicks. And with Aline he'd had a dream of the future. Trying to get a decent job, build a family . . . That was as far as he got.

"Casinos. Hell, *Indians* putting up casinos. Brilliant. They had nothing. Now they got everything. Except the Navajos. No casinos for them. Missed all the fun along with the moola. They're above it all." He shook his head, leaned toward him.

"How about a little game to pass the time? Five hundred dollars. No, make it a thousand. I've made something of myself in the world. I got money to burn. Hell, I'm a gambling man—it's in my blood. Lost my wife—too many trips on account of it. Too many trips to Vegas. Afraid I'd bankrupt us. No faith. Here's your chance."

"I got nothing to bet."

"Sure you do. You got that lease."

He shook his head. "Don't even know if anybody owns that land now. It's worthless. Besides I just left it behind."

"Okay, no worry. We can look into it. There are records. We'll just bet on it to have something to bet."

Hawkins shook his head.

"What else?"

He shrugged. "My truck." He wasn't serious.

"That piece of junk? What've got in your pockets?"

He took out his billfold and opened it. "See—nothing in it." He couldn't help smiling. Even his driver's license was about to expire.

"What's in your pockets?"

"Nothing."

"Nothing? I'm here to make something out of nothing. I've done it before—more than once. I can do it again." Big grin—triumphant.

Hawkins tried to look at him squarely and not get caught in his net. What was he trying to make out of his nothing? As though he were making everything up as he went along.

"Looks to me you got something in that front pocket."

"A stone—that's all."

"A stone, huh? A lucky stone. Let's see it."

"No," Hawkins said, "I don't gamble."

"Of course you do—you're here, aren't you? You got nothing, you're gambling everything. Show me that stone."

Crazy. Almost as though Thornton would pull out a gun and make him give it up, not because it was worth anything but just to show he could take it if he wanted it. Hawkins was thrown for a loop. Something had risen in him for a brief moment. The great rush of energy the snake had awakened. Like a vision—but where it was supposed to take him? How was he was to forge ahead and live? The voice wasn't offering any answers. It seemed to have abandoned him.

His nothing was a rusting truck and the clothes on his back. He'd been carried along in a momentum and had now awakened to the light of the morning. He was left to his own devices. If he had a stake in the future, he hardly knew where it lay. He could only try for a new start. He still had his obligation. The stone weighed heavily in his pocket. But he would still keep his promise. Climb up to Pueblo

Alto—not miss the path this time—and lay it on the wall. Yes, he could do that—let him fulfill his obligation and be free.

"Come on," Everett was insisting. "Give me a look-see." Bending forward, holding out his hand.

He could almost feel himself dissolving in Thornton's leer, the narrowing eyes, the yellow irises and dark pupils. Coyote eyes. "I want to see that stone."

He should just get up and walk away, but something held him there. He reached into his pocket and drew out the stone. It felt cold in his hand. He turned it over, keeping his fingers curled as though to protect it.

"I can't see it that way," Thornton said, taking it out of his hand. He held it up to the light. "Nice colors."

"It's not worth anything."

"Then I can just throw it in the bushes, can't I?" He looked at Hawkins narrowly. "No, I don't believe it. It's your lucky stone. I can feel it," he said, clasping his fist around it. "Tell you what. We'll play for it."

"No, I don't gamble." His mouth was dry.

"If you win," Everett said, his voice like honey, "you'll be a man who can stand up on his own. Not owe anything to anybody. You'll have a whole world before you—golden as the sunrise."

His vision seemed to darken. "And if I lose," Hawkins said.

"Then I'll tell you what you've lost."

What kind of answer was this? Everything seemed to be swept away before his eyes, whatever world had existed in all its changes. Past and future. And the present was like quicksand he was stepping into. Only the stone existed. All meaning seemed to lie in it. And his posession of it hung in the balance. It was almost as though Thornton had won it already.

Thornton brought out a little black case and opened it carefully. A pair of dice lay inside. "See these—one of a kind. I collect 'em. Got some beauties in my office. Knock your socks off. Pyramid shaped, all colors. Six-sided. Egyptian, Chinese. Pipped and square. Aren't these the beauties?

They were square, with circles containing brown and white triangles, the dots in the center. Hawkins turned them over in his palm. These, too, reminded him of rattlesnakes.

Then Everett set down a large piece of turquoise. Hawkins had never seen anything like it. A deep aquamarine, marked by black lines and black patches that divided the surface into various shapes, like rocks emerging from a sea. "It's my luck," Thornton said. "I take it everywhere. You got to carry your own luck," he said, as if he were conveying a secret. "And I got mine."

And where was his? Thornton wasn't giving it up. Hawkins wondered. If the stone meant anything after all—it was out of his hands. What did it mean in another's?

"Don't worry, I play for the fun of it—maybe that's why I almost never lose." He looked over at Hawkins, smiled. "Life's a game. Win some, lose some. I've won plenty. Because I concentrate. Maybe some of my luck will rub off on you."

It was hardly reassuring. Thornton gave a little chuckle that suggested the opposite. "Here," he said, handing Hawkins the dice. "You first. At least three rounds. A chance for the loser. Blow on them for luck."

Hawkins threw the dice and looked down at a seven.

"Beginner's luck. Throw another and you'll be the big winner."

Everything depending on the roll of the dice. It wasn't clear what he was doing or could do to keep things from spinning out from under him.

When Thornton handed him the dice again, he had the sense he was stepping outside the circle of whatever power he had and entering another territory. Here they were, the two of them concentrating on the dice, as though each was trying to breathe into them certain numbers to bring a reality. He watched the way Everett picked up the dice, held them in his hand as though to fix the numbers, then gave a quick roll down to the table and then opened his eyes to the results, jutting out his lower lip. This time Thonton threw a five—then Hawkins picked up the dice and threw. He was looking down at a single dot on each of the dice.

"Snake eyes," Everett announced. "You're out of this one."

The snakes on the dice had uncoiled, it seemed, and he was looking into the eyes that had defeated him.

And then something happened that pulled time out of its socket. The dice game seemed to go on for an eternity, he throwing round after round, looking at the numbers, trying to control the spin, but losing, always losing. He knew what he'd known all along, that he had gambled away his life. Thornton had won.

"Here, you can have your wretched stone, tossing it to him. It's not worth shit."

Hawkins was looking up into a grinning face, then at a figure that grew more momentous as he watched.

"I won. You work for me now," Thornton told him. "You'll go around and convince those Indians to let us on their reservation and let us stake our claims. No more nonsense. The world's out there waiting. And just suppose one of those Indians ended up in a ditch somewhere. Pick a man with lots of kin. Might change a few minds."

"No," Hawkins said. "No."

"I'm the one in charge here, and you—" he said, tapping Hawkins on the chest, "—you are my employee. Doing a little hands-on." The idea tickled him. "And you'll be glad to do my bidding."

As if he weren't already undone, Thornton's shape began to change before his eyes. The figure took on greater bulk, as though he'd balloon into the beyond—fill the sky. He loomed over Hawkins with massive head and shoulders, thick hair and cavernous eyes. At the same moment they were occupying a different space. Time had reversed itself, opening a crack: the past was the present, and they'd been sucked backward into it. In the rush of appearances. Hawkins hardly knew what he was seeing.

The pueblo had taken on a new kind of splendor, as he found himself in the plaza of Pueblo Bonito in its former state. He was standing beside one of the great kivas, now covered with vigas and plastered over, so that it held its mysteries intact. The pueblo stood nobly in its several storeys, the top roofed over, the outside bricks of the rooms covered with plaster. The great rock that had broken loose and caused one end of the building to fall into ruin was intact, back in place. The plaza was filled with people trading their goods, setting up cooking pots and households in the nearby pueblos. Several neighboring tribes, distinguished by their dress, had come to prepare for the ceremonies about to take place. They wore their necklaces of beads, shells and turquoise, and head-dresses of eagle and macaw feathers.

Hawkins stood in the midst of all this activity, uncertain where he should go. Children pointed at him and spoke excitedly to their parents, but they either ignored him or did not see him.

The other figure in their midst claimed their attention. He towered over the others, who were barely five feet tall, exhorting, challenging, cajoling. They looked at him with wonder—where had he come from? From the mountains, from the sky? From some land near the water?

"I see gamblers among you," he announced, holding up a pair of bone dice in one hand and gaming sticks in the other. "And I can win any game you want to play. Win any contest." Did they want to test their skill and courage? he challenged them. "I'll take you on."

The men could only laugh at him. They knew dice—they had their antelope bones, their red and white squares, and they were practiced. They exchanged glances. Those who lived there in the canyon had to impress the visitors or they would lose respect. The stranger would already have won if they didn't rise to the occasion.

The men stood talking in little knots as Hawkins watched. Then several figures appeared, naked, painted in white, dancing around among the crowd. People laughed at their antics, particularly the women, as the clowns tried to capture first one, then another. They seized a couple of young boys, carried them off amid a great deal of laughter, and dumped them unceremoniously into the nearby stream.

But the stranger had their attention. "Do you have any wealth or not? Are you just pretending—full of pride?" The clowns puffed themselves up and strode in front of the crowd, mimicking the gambler. The gambler waved them away—as if they were pieces of chaff. Barely men at all. For the rest, the real men—what stakes would they put up? They were rich in ornaments, weren't they?—turquoise beads, eagle and macaw feathers, shells that had come from the land near the waves? "What do you have to show?"

One of the clowns held out his genitals and marched around, provoking laughter, then retreated with his hands covering them, as though they'd disappeared.

Watching the display, Hawkins feeling his own sense of defeat, his lack of will to resist, tried to hang on from one moment to the next. A restlessness seized the crowd. Something was out of joint. The clowns were not only making fun of the gambler but making fun of them as well. Why didn't the chiefs walk away? The clowns were appealing to the crowd as they gamboled in their midst. Why were they so eager to please a stranger? Why and why?

The gambler was casting a spell. Hawkins could see how he was bringing it off, had brought it off with him. How one by one the chiefs of the various clans—the Bear, the Corn, the Rabbit, the Snake, the Antelope—took their ornaments and set them on a deerskin in front of the gambler, who urged them on. Why? and Why? the clowns kept making the rounds with their appeal, and the people began to question and argue.

"Are you men or not?" the gambler challenged them, striding about. "Aren't you equal to the game?"

That was the kicker, Hawkins thought. It spoke to the blood; it had aroused him. As if it were something you could stand on. He had seen it all before, there with Drew and the others. He could tell that one of the chiefs, maybe chief of the Antelope clan, resisted strongly. He spoke to the others.

"Do you need a special council before you can think for yourselves? Before you decide? Are you babes in arms?" All eyes were on them. They would give their answer later in the afternoon.

In the end, the Antelope chief must have been overruled, and though he kept shaking his head no, the others were putting him forward to be their challenger.

He was a powerful-looking man and seemed to be held in great respect by those around him. When he did step forward, he did so proudly, though one of the clowns, making one more effort, rolled over as though to trip him up. There was general laughter. For a moment it appeared everything would break apart into the ridiculous.

"This is a man who doesn't know how to gamble," the gambler said indulgently. "But then he's like a child afraid of his shadow."

The chief set down a notable piece of turquoise, a piece that had been highly polished. It would be a great sacrifice if he were to lose it, Hawkins thought. It was even more beautiful than Thornton's. Perhaps it had been a choice piece to protect him from harm and bring good fortune, The gambler picked up the turquoise and turned it in his hand. No doubt it had caught his eye with its rich color. "Ah," he said. "I'll take that for my lucky piece."

And what would the gambler bet? "Myself," he said. "This body, these arms and legs—for whatever use you put me to." The crowd that had been gathering now regarded him with astonishment. What sort of man would gamble his life? They turned to one another, unable to comprehend. It was against nature, this pride. The man was a fool or else a man so used to winning he must be . . . what must he be? It was a question. Yet he could also lose. And what would he do then? He stood among them without the least sign of fear, but with a confidence that could only win respect.

Indeed the gambler seemed no mere man, but a being who stood beyond them, more than man—in touch with another world. The Chief went up to meet his challenge. The dice favored one, then the other—back and forth, as though they had the same power over luck, but then as the crowd waited breathlessly, a cloud came over the sun. And quite before they knew what was happening, they watched the dice fall. The gambler had won the turquoise. They rocked back on their heels. A terrible thing for the Antelope Chief to lose. His protection. His tie to good fortune. The shadow that fell into their courtyard grew more dense; it crossed in front of their eyes, and they were like shadows.

Hawkins could barely see their expressions, but he could tell they must be afraid of what might happen next. The clan chief had to win it back—it must be a sacred amulet. It must madden them that this boastful stranger had won, that he had such power over them. At the back of the crowd, the muttering began among them, as the gambler stood there with the object in his hand, a triumphant gleam in his eye, stood there with the deep satisfaction that he had won something that the chief could hardly bear to lose. Nor could the rest of the tribe bear to see it lost.

"So now I've got a lucky piece," the gambler said.

There was a shift. What had stood in balance began tipping in another direction, for a now a man stood naked without his protection.

Now they were held in the suspense of their wavering concern.

"But I'll give you a chance—you can win it back," the gambler said.

The Antelope Chief once again took his place and prepared for better luck despite his disadvantage.

Though the Chief carried the experience of his years, he must, Hawkins thought, feel the pressure of the crowd around him and the need for concentration. The people seemed to draw in a single breath, holding it with one mind concentrating on winning. But again the dice went against the Chief, and the pile of ornaments, their treasures, went to the gambler.

They stood in disarray. Yet they could not step away from their losses and go home to their defeat. One by one, they brought out their drums and flutes and sacred stones from the kivas. They could not look at one another or acknowledge what they were doing. They had to win—surely the gods would not desert them. Hawkins wanted desperately to warn them of his own loss. To speak of how they had been betrayed. For what had made him take up the challenge was the thing that had taken him the wrong way before. Even though it would have been hard, he could refused to hand over the stone, could have stepped away, as he should have done with Drew and Mackey, but like them, he had something to prove.

With horror he watched as the clansmen gambled their property, then their wives and children, who stood with stony faces as they were made to leave their families to become the stranger's property.

Suddenly, the people were struck by full impact of what they'd done. Everything gone. The only stake left was themselves. The gambler was filled with relish to continue the contest. Things had gone entirelyhis way, and he held up the piece of turquoise that had been his luck.

The men suggested another contest with squares painted red on one side, white on the other. Whoever threw down the most white squares would win. They chose one of the young warriors to defeat the stranger. His hands were quick and accurate with the bow. The odds were against him, but he stood firmly, ready to serve the tribe.

And they had to watch luck abandon them one final time. Those who had ruled the pueblos were now slaves—the shamans and priests who kept their stations and charted the course of sun and moon; the chiefs of the clans; the farmers and hunters; women and children. The gambler would rule over them now.

Hawkins watched the future unfold like a reel playing in his mind, time spinning out and away until years and centuries passed through his mind like a prophecy. In the days following, Chaco Canyon had never known such activity. It soon became clear that the Great Gambler had come to them with something in mind: to build and keep on building. More pueblos, more kivas, more roads that connected to other pueblos. The men had to go far for the wood for the posts and vigas, and how they managed to bring them back is a mystery. They worked day in, day out—up at dawn, busy until sunset. They had little time for anything else, for the darkness brought only their weariness and aching bones.

Meanwhile, the Great Gambler enjoyed their wives, as he fattened with ease and pleasure.

More and more, tribesmen and women came for trade and ceremony. It was a center, perhaps the center of the earth. The news spread north and south. The more the people of Chaco built, the more impressive the city became—kivas, pueblos, roads, all kept in their relations with sun, moon, and constellations, the way light and shadows were cast at the time of equinox and solstice.

A center of power. More and more power as people came to the dozens of kivas and held their ceremonies and traded their goods, the plazas filled with their dances and chanting. But the landscape was changing. Forests had been cut down for the wood to build the pueblos and kivas; the wash was going dry, for the rain was less plentiful despite the ceremonies. The clouds would gather and darken, but only a few drops fell. The Day Keepers, who observed the rising and revolutons of sun and moon so that crops could be planted and gathered at the right times, could not prevent the growing scarcities of food.

But the Great Gambler was not dismayed. "It's all as it should be," he announced triumphantly. "Now you are ready to learn the great secret. You have built the great kivas with all the ceremonies held there. All the prayers and offerings have built up a power unknown in the world before. No longer will there be this drought, the lack of food. We can now control the weather."

It was unimaginable—yet things were going badly. The shamans and elders were filled with dismay. And what of the gods? they wanted to know.

The Great Gambler laughed. "No longer needed," he said. "We're in charge now. They're as worn out as last year's calendar. The power belongs to us for what we've done. They can spend all their time playing dice." He laughed with delight . He called on the chiefs and the priests to put their knowledge together.

But before he could continue, half a dozen clowns descended from the pueblos, stripped to their nakedness, even though the weather was freezing. "What are you doing?" they demanded of the Gambler. "We're the ones supposed to turn things upside down and inside out." Now they went about the crowd, taking women's things to wear around their necks, trying to carry the Gambler's women off by force. Then they enacted moments of shame—when they had tried to show off their prowess to someone's disadvantage or acted with stubbornness and discontent when they didn't have their way.

The crowd began to look at them as if in a mirror. And Hawkins was there with them, joined in the same recognition. All of them had allowed themselves to be used and turned to another's purposes. Only the clowns had kept their sense of the right order of things. The chiefs had given away what should have been theirs and watched it turned inside out. The Gambler would take his power beyond all they knew—beyond nature itself.

"But how do we know you still have power?" one of the clowns asked, "that you have power over the sun and rain."

"Look around," the Great Gambler said imperturbably. "See what you've built for me. Now all the power is here in this canyon, ready to be used.

"You haven't gambled with us," the clown said. "A clown is never a slave."

The Gambler roared with laughter. "What do you have to gamble? Do you really think you can win over me? You're like this stone," he said, picking one up and throwing it at one of the mongrel dogs that nosed about at the edge of the crowd. The dog yelped and crept away.

"My nose," said the clown. "I'll bet my nose. I can make it grow longer or shorter."

"Which means, if you lose, I can remove it from your face."

"I can do without it. I've already smelled things out."

The Gambler pulled out the piece of turquoise he'd won from the Antelope Chief. "You think you can beat this?" he said.

But just at that moment two crows flew down, flapping their wings in his face, pecking at him, while he flailed and tried to push them off. "Get away, get away, you damned birds." Perhaps he let go of the turquoise as he struggled against them. Or perhaps the crows snatched it from his hands. For they were attracted by bright objects. But when they flew off, the Great Gambler no longer had it.

The crowd had been watching, some with wonder, the clowns with laughter. Hawkins let out a cheer.

"You think you can still win?" the clowns taunted.

The Great Gambler managed a laugh, though he was disheveled and he was wiping blood from the scratches on his face. "You think I can't? Well, think again," he yelled. "I won before I had the turquoise. And I can always win without it." Scornfully he threw a set of antelope bone dice and stood daring anyone there to step up and challenge him. Perhaps he thought no one would.

But Hawkins had a feeling, at first just a faint suggestion that something had shifted and changed in the atmosphere, that the tribe, beaten down for so long was coming together with the force of will.

"Inside out and outside in. Up is down and down is up," the clowns chanted. As the others watched, one of them danced in, swept up the antelope bone dice, and to the Great Gambler's surprise won all three rounds. The crowd let out a great yell. Since he had won, the clown challenged the Gambler to a game of red and white squares. When the Gambler tossed them up it was though creatures of the air must have turned the colors so that he would lose. It was different with the hoop game that followed. The wives and children were at stake, and their lives hung in the balance. When the Gambler's hoop was caught in the string set up for it, a groan went through the crowd, but just as the Gambler turned toward them in triumph, the hoop gave a little jerk, as though something were moving inside it, and it rolled down to the ground.

A great roar went up from the crowd as the wives and children raced back to their husbands and fathers, and the Gambler simply stood waving his arms and trying to yell above the chaos. They must have had help. What had been turned upside down had been righted. Hawkins could tell. The forces of earth and air had assisted them, had allowed them to put things back in balance. Only now they lacked water for crops and the trees that helped to bring the rain. And it became clear that the people would have to leave the Canyon and search for a new home and a new beginning. For the damage had been done and there was no going back. Hawkins walked aimlessly through the pueblo as people were beginning to seal up the doorways of their dwelling and gather what they needed to take with them for their pilgrimage.

He was looking at the unpredictable, which could save you or kill you. Or send you on your way. In some sense he'd been saved before. And he knew, too, that he'd been cheated, that a mist had covered his eyes when he met Thornton's challenge. Once more he'd forgotten to walk away. When he returned to what the day was offering him, the stone was giving off its colors in his mind. If it could assist him, if there was any power there . . . if she who put it in his hand could help him . . . His life still lay in fragments. He could hardly do what the stone required. He had possessed only the naked entity. If a stone was anything, it had some kind of meaning in the scheme of things. And it made no difference that he'd had to make its discovery.

"Wait," Hawkins said to the man sitting opposite him, who had won the right to rule over him. "I still have the stone, since you threw it back to me. It's the one thing I have to bet." With great effort he pushed aside his fear. "It still has a power."

"I don't believe it?" Thornton said. "So you want to bet again." He laughed. "Well, I'm a gambler. But I know the probabilities."

Hawkins held out the stone. He could feel Everett's contempt.

"You really think you have changed your luck?

He brought out the turquoise. "Against this—against me?"

Hawkins took the dice and threw a seven.

"What d'you know," Thornton said. "I didn't think those dice would ever fail me." He looked over at Hawkins. "I think we got one more thing we can bet on. Like I say, I gamble for fun," he said, "and when it isn't fun anymore . . ."

Hawkins stood up, not to be prevented by whatever was veiled in the threat. Perhaps he did indeed carry a pistol on him. "Keep your turquoise," he said, as he turned away. "It's all yours."

"Wait, wait, you son-of-a-bitch," Thornton yelled after him. "I still have two more chances."

Hawkins didn't look back. He reached his truck and climbed in. He had the stone. It was his now. It only remained for him to make the climb up to Pueblo Alto and find a good place for it.

Gladys Swan has published three novels, *Carnival for the Gods*, (Vintage Contemporaries Series), *Ghost Dance: A Play of Voices*, (LSU Press, nominated for the PEN/Faulkner Award), and *A Dark Gamble*, as well as seven collections of short fiction. Her poetry and essays, and short stories have appeared in many literary magazines and anthologies. Much of her work is set in New Mexico, where she grew up. Though she has spent most of her career as a writer, she has devoted much of her time during the last two decades to painting and exploring the creative process. She was the first writer since the inception of the Vermont Studio Center to receive a fellowship for a residency in painting. She also received a fellowship from the Lilly Endowment for a year's study of Inuit art and mythology and a Fulbright Award as a writer-in-residence in Yugoslavia. Her paintings have appeared as the cover art for various literary magazines and books, including the most recently published, *The Tiger's Eye: New & Selected Stories*. She has twice been a Guest Writer at the Vermont Studio Center and has held residencies at Yaddo, the Chateau de Lavigny in Switzerland. the Fimdacion Valparaiso in Spain and others. She has taught literature and creative writing at various colleges and universities, notably, in the MFA Program at the Vermont College of the Arts and at the University of Missouri-Columbia. She received an Honorary Doctorate of Humane Letters from Western New Mexico University and gave the commencement address. *The Carnival Quintet*, an outgrowth of her first novel, is being published by Kiwai Media in Paris. The first volume, *Carnival for the Gods*, appeared in September, 2014. She has done the cover paintings for the series.